eMAGIC LOGIC

Virtual
Instruments
a user's guide

Stephen Bennett

PC Publishing

PC Publishing
Export House
130 Vale Road
Tonbridge
Kent TN9 1SP
UK

Tel 01732 770893
Fax 01732 770268
email info@pc-publishing.com
web site http://www.pc-publishing.com

First published 2003

© PC Publishing

ISBN 1 870775 848

British Library Cataloguing in Publication Data
A catalogue record for this book is available from the British Library

Cover design by Michelle Raki

Printed in Great Britain by Biddles, Guildford

Preface

The high-quality Virtual Instruments built into Logic Audio really do make the 'studio in a box' a reality right now. It's possible to create a piece of music and record it just using Emagic Logic and the plug-ins – no external gear needed! And if you think the results won't be up there with the 'Pros' - think again. These are the very people who are using Logic's Virtual Instruments to produce hit records – and you can too. The Virtual Instruments make previously expensive or inaccessible sounds available to every Logic user. For example, the EVB3 is a brilliant recreation of a *recorded* Hammond B3 with Leslie – in fact, several Hammonds and Leslies. While Virtual Instruments cannot recreate the feel, smell, cost and unreliability of the real thing, even an expert would be hard pressed to tell them apart from a 'smoking' B3. The EVP88 electric piano instrument even has a 'virtual' lid to keep out 'virtual' dust!

The book details the parameters of all the Virtual Instruments within Logic along with their effects and use. This combined with 'how to' examples and tips makes it an essential accessory to using Logic's Virtual Instruments.

Dedication

For Mary & William.

Acknowledgements

I'd like to thank Phil Chapman at PC Publishing, Dave Marshall at Sound Technology, The Logic Users Group, Emagic and the cats at Chaos.

Contents

(U/V). Using the EVOC as a polysynth. The EVOC 20 TO tracking oscillator. The EVOC 20 FB filter bank.

Introduction

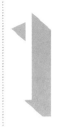

E ver since the computer was first used to make music, the idea of the 'virtu-al studio' or 'studio in a box' has become a kind of holy grail in the music technology world. First computers were used to control MIDI devices. Then, as processor power increased, software was developed to record audio and then to process that audio with 'virtual' effects units. Now, with the latest generation of computers, powerful 'virtual instruments' have become available. These instru-ments range from emulations of classic synthesisers to more 'out there' software. It's now possible to record and mix complete tracks, then burn them to CD on a portable computer with no external hardware.

Emagic Logic comes with several virtual instruments supplied free, while others are 'purchase on demand'. These instruments are Logic Audio only – although Emagic have made available several cut down VST versions of some of them. They range from classic emulations to powerful multi-format synthesisers. They are sim-ilar to 'normal' VST virtual Instruments (VSTi), but because they are integrated into Logic Audio they often use a lot less CPU power than third party VSTi's. How many Logic Audio Virtual Instruments you can use in a song is dependent on the power of your computer. The beauty of this is that you can have multiple instances of the same Virtual Instrument in your song. You want 10 virtual monosynths? No prob-lem! Six electric pianos? Easy peasy!

This book is a guide to using the Logic Instruments. It takes you from purchase and installation to using those instruments. It's full of tips and tricks to help you get the most out of Logic's Virtual Instruments.

The book also assumes you are familiar with Logic Audio software and your com-puter's operating system.

It's worth reading the book straight through first, as information given in one chapter is often relevant to another. For example, the chapters on the ESM and ES1 contain information on synthesisers that will come in useful when you read about the ES2, EXS24 and EVOC 20.

Purchase and installation

With version 5 of Logic, Emagic introduced the XSKey USB Dongle. Like the old dongle which was used with previous versions of Logic Audio, the XSkey protects the program from the unauthorised copying and use of Logic Audio. Unlike the old dongle, the codes you need to run Logic Audio, along with any Logic Audio Virtual Instruments you have purchased, are stored on the dongle itself. CD or floppy disk authorisation is no longer needed – all this is taken care of by the XSkey. You are free to copy and backup Logic Audio software, but you can't run the program without the XSkey connected. You could, for example, have the Logic Audio software on a desktop and portable computer and just swap the XSkey between the machines to run Logic Audio.

While the codes you need to run the Logic Virtual Instruments are contained in the XSkey itself, the actual Virtual Instrument software is embedded within the Logic Audio program. The box you get from the shop just contains a CD containing the latest version of Logic, samples or other extra software. You'll also get a card with the temporary authorisation codes you need to get up and running right away, along with information on how to obtain permanent codes. The advantage of this is that when Logic Audio is upgraded, so are the Virtual Instruments, thus making sure that you have all the correct and latest versions.

Purchasing Logic Virtual Instruments

You purchase these from your Logic dealer or reseller. You'll get a box which contains, depending on which instruments you buy, a manual, CD and registration information.

Installing Logic Virtual Instruments

Make sure the XSkey is plugged into a USB port on your computer.

- Load Logic
- Run the XSkey Authorisation program. Where this is Located depends upon your platform.

  * Macintosh OSX – In the Logic Platinum menu when running Logic
  * Macintosh OS9 – In the Apple menu when running Logic
  * Windows – In the Help menu when running Logic

- You'll see a list of current Logic Virtual Instruments.

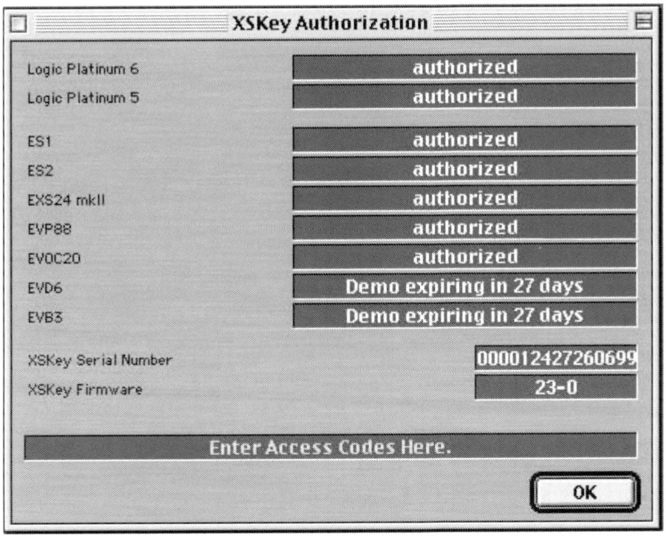

Figure 2.1

On the Registration card in the box will be a temporary access code (Type B). Just type this code into the box in the window. This will give you use of the Virtual Instruments until your permanent codes arrive (Type A).

Obtaining permanent access codes (Type A)

There are two ways to do this. Either send off the registration card and wait for the code to arrive by mail. Or, if you want the code more quickly, register online at the Emagic website. The registration card will have details of the correct web addresses. When you receive the permanent access codes you then enter them into XSkey authorisation window in exactly the same way as the temporary codes.

You can also use Virtual instruments in Demo mode to try them out before purchase. This is covered in more detail in Chapter 3

Your Emagic Logic Virtual Instruments are now ready for use! The next chapter covers their general use within Logic.

Common parameters

E magic Logic's Virtual Instruments have many parameters in common. Here's a handy list.

- Clicking and dragging a knob to the right or left changes the value. Holding down the CTRL key when you drag makes the movement finer.
- Presets for the Virtual Instruments are stored in the Plug-in preset folder in the Logic audio folder. Each Instrument has its own folder (Figure 3.1).
- These presets are accessed from the pull down menu (Figure 3.2).

Figure 3.1

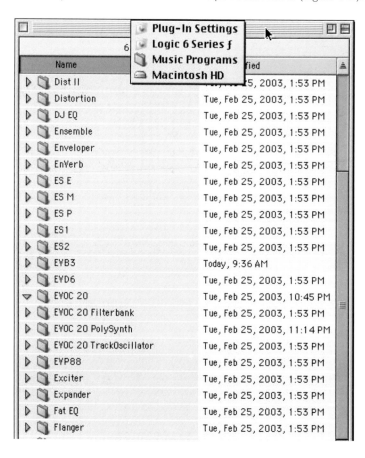

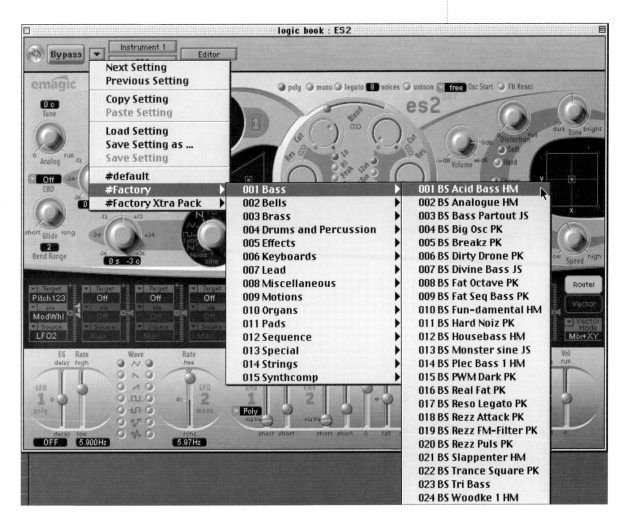

Figure 3.2

- You should save your own presets here too. You can make sub folders in the folders for your sounds (Figure 3.3).

Figurre 3.3

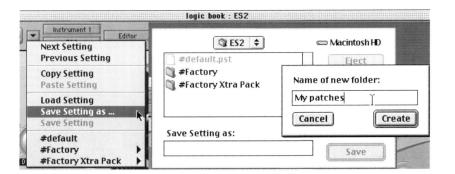

- You can use Key commands to change the presets (Figure 3.4).

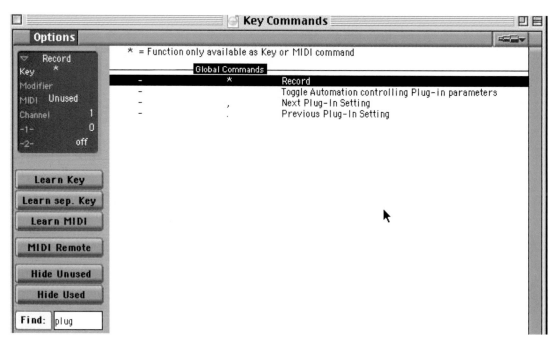

Figure 3.4

- Logic Audio displays the preset name where possible on the Arrange page (Figure 3.5).

Figure 3.5

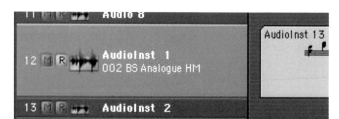

- All Logic Plug-ins have a non graphical interface accessed from the pull down menu. Sometimes it's easier to see what's going on with the Instrument here (Figure 3.6).

Figure 3.6

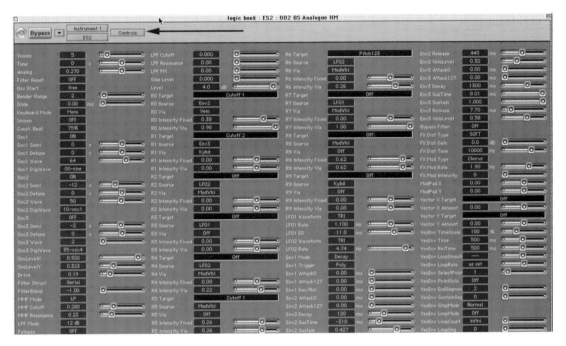

- You record a Virtual Instrument in the same way as you record MIDI data. The recording can be edited in the same fashion, and you can play back a sequence recorded with a Virtual Instrument with a MIDI device and vice-versa.
- If a Virtual Instrument has a parameter box with numbers in it, you can hold down the mouse button over the box and drag the mouse up and down to change values (Figure 3.7).
- If a Virtual Instrument has a parameter box with other values in it, you can hold down the mouse button over the box pop up menu appears (Figure 3.8).

Figure 3.7

Figure 3.8

Using Logic Virtual Instruments

Figure 4.1 (above)

Figure 4.2 (right)
Creaing an Instrument Object

ogic Virtual Instruments are used within the Logic by being inserted into a special kind of Audio object – the Instrument object.

Several of these objects are created automatically when you run Logic Audio for the first time. You can also create new Instrument objects in the Environment whenever you need them.

Creating Instrument objects

- Open an Environment window.
- Select New>Audio object from the pull down menu.
- Double click on the icon created.

Select the Instrument. In the parameter box, choose the next Instrument from the menu. Instrument numbers already existing in the song are highlighted in bold. In this example, there are already 13 Instrument objects in this song.

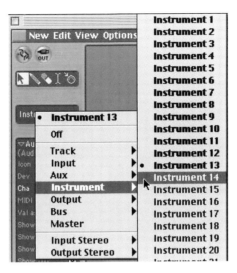

Figure 4.2

To Insert a Logic Virtual Instrument

Click and hold on the I/O box as in Figure 4.3. A pull down menu allows you to select Logic Virtual Instruments. There are Mono, Stereo and Multi Channel versions of the Virtual Instruments. Not all Instruments will appear in all menus.

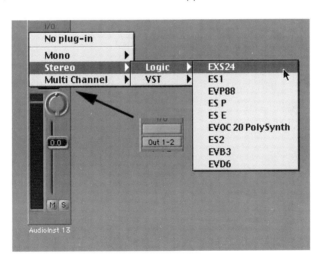

Figure 4.3

- Mono Instruments have a single or monophonic output. The Audio object will be a mono one and the pan control will move the sound field to the left or right, or around the surround stage if surround output is selected for the output of the Instruments.
- Stereo Instruments have two outputs and the pan control balances the left and right outputs.

- Multi Channel Instruments can send several outputs to separate Aux audio objects, so each channel can be processed separately. These are covered in detail in the chapter on the EXS24 Sampler Virtual Instrument, Chapter 15.

Figure 4.4

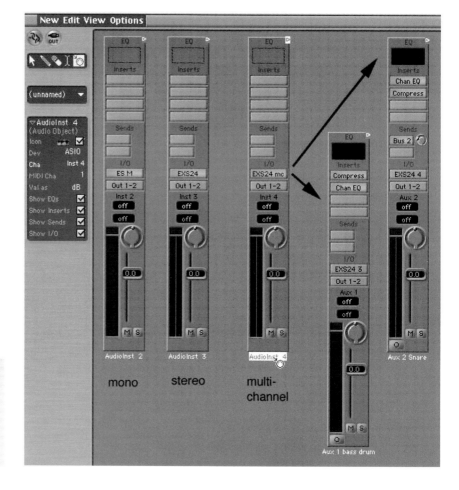

The selected Virtual Instrument opens as a plug-in window (Figure 4.5).

Figure 4.5

You can of course insert effects plug-ins in the usual way. Also, you can send the output of Virtual Instruments to Busses or Auxes in exactly the same way you can for normal Audio objects.

Playing and recording Virtual Instruments

Virtual Instruments are selected in the Arrange page in exactly the same way MIDI Instruments are.

Click and hold on the Instrument's name column and select the required Virtual Instrument (Figure 4.6).

Figure 4.6

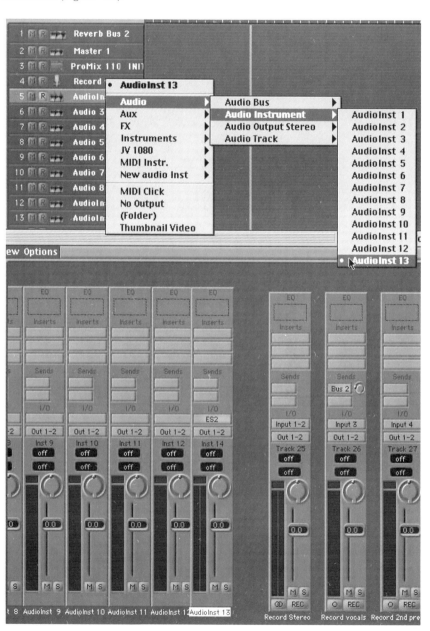

Now record into Logic Audio in the usual way. Data is recorded as MIDI information which can be edited in any of Logic's editors (Figure 4.7).

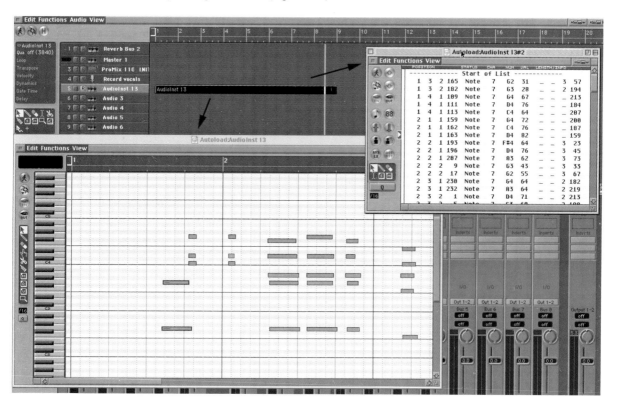

Figure 4.7

You can also record the movements of any of the Virtual Instruments controls into Logic's automation system. This is one of the beauties of using the Emagic's virtual Instruments – all the data recorded is described by name rather than some obscure controller number.

Figure 4.9

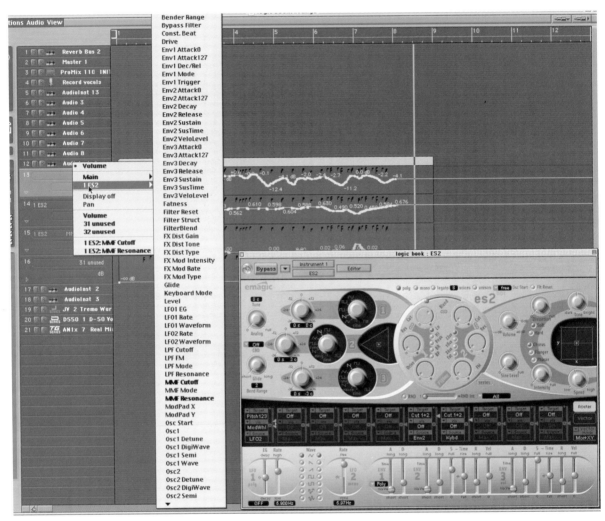

Latency

Latency exhibits itself with Virtual Instruments as the delay between playing a MIDI controller, such as a keyboard, and hearing the sound produced by the Virtual Instrument. It's the time taken for the MIDI data to enter the computer, pass to the Virtual Instrument and then out through the sound hardware. Most Audio hardware device drivers allow you to select different latencies as buffer sizes. Usually, the lower the size the faster the response. Be warned, however, that the lower the buffer size the higher the strain on the computers CPU. Select the lowest buffer that allows you to play the Virtual Instrument responsively.

Tip

If you insert a Virtual Instrument that you have not purchased, the Virtual instrument opens in demo mode. From this point on, you can try out the Instrument in fully functional demo mode to see if you like it. You can see how long you have left of the demo in the XSkey authorisation window

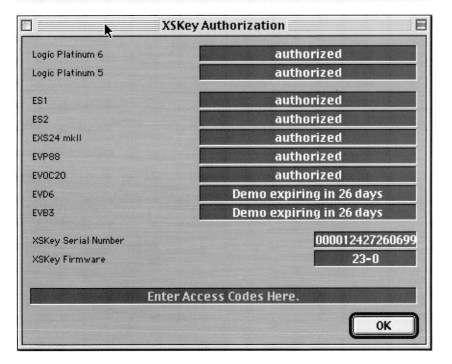

Figure 4.10

How many Virtual Instruments can I use?

The short answer is as many as you want up to the limit of your computers CPU power! However, your version of Logic Audio may have a limit of 32 or 64 Instrument objects.

You can free up CPU power by recording the Virtual Instrument as an Audio track. This is covered in more detail in Appendix 1.

Virtual synthesis

The synthesisers in Logic are computer generated emulations of real life instruments. However, because their sounds are generated digitally, their stability and feature lists are far superior to their real life counterparts – not to say far cheaper to buy!

In 'real' analogue hardware the different sections of synthesisers are controlled by voltages so oscillators are called Voltage controlled oscillators (VCO), filters are called Voltage controlled filters (VCF) and so on. This terminology has come with us into the virtual age even though the control is now digital.

Though the EVOC, ES1 and ES2 are fairly complex virtual synthesisers, the free ESM, ESP and ESE are great sounding basic instruments and are a good place to start with synthesis.

Info

Different synthesiser manufacturers often describe the same feature on an Instrument in different terms. This can lead to confusion. Throughout this book the following terms are used

Voices – the number of simultaneous keys that will sound. For example, if the Voices parameter is set to '1', only one note will sound at a time – the synth will be monophonic. If it's set to '5', five notes will sound at a time.

Preset – this is a sound on the virtual instrument. These are stored on disk and accessed via the usual plug-in menu.

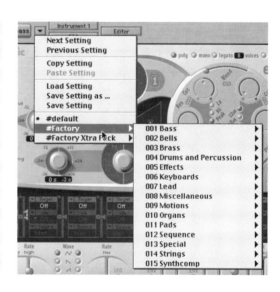

Though they may vary in several areas, Logic's virtual synthesisers all have similar sound generation and shaping functions. These are detailed below.

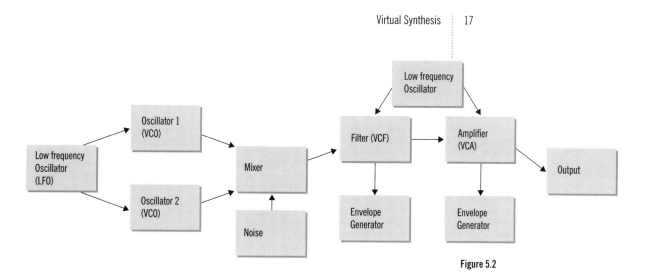

Figure 5.2

Oscillators (VCO) – the sound sources

Simple analogue synthesisers have at least one oscillator that generates waveforms that are the basic sound sources of a synthesiser. Typically, the waveforms generated are;

- Sine – a pure tone used for generating organ type sounds
- Triangle – similar to a sine wave in tone but with more harmonics. It's usually used for 'flute-like' sounds.
- Sawtooth – traditionally used to simulate string-like tones.
- Square – has a 'hollow' quality and is often used to produce clarinet-like tones.

The pulse width (distance between peaks) of a square wave can be changed. At low percentages the wave sounds thin at high percentages the sound is more nasal (Figure 5.7).

If the synthesiser has several oscillators these can be mixed together to form more complex waveforms. You can also detune these slightly against each other to 'fatten' up the sound. In addition, there are often 'sub' tones that can be added to beef up thin sounds or different waveforms can be mixed together in a single oscillator.

Oscillators can also have digital waveforms. These could be samples of acoustic sounds or digitally generated waveforms with unusual and complex harmonics. As these can be mixed together in multi-oscillator systems, the possibilities for generating complex sound sources are huge.

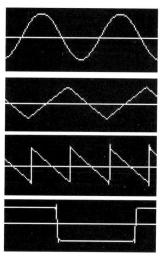

Figures 5.3 – 5.6 (above)
Sine, triangle, sawtooth and square waveforms. The waveforms shown are a little distorted. They came from a 'real life' synthesiser. These distortions can often add character to an instrument

Figure 5.7
The pulse width (distance between peaks) of a square wave can be changed

The pitch of the oscillator is usually set in octave steps and the actual note defined by the MIDI note value of the MIDI controller.

Some synthesisers also have a noise source. This is often used for effects or creating atmospheric sounds.

Mixer

If there's more than one oscillator or there is a noise generator, these can be mixed together and their levels set before passing the sound onto the filter.

Filters (VCF)

A filter is used as a kind of tone control to modify the sound of the oscillators. They usually have two controls.

- Cutoff – defines the frequency where the filtering effect happens.
- Resonance – emphasises the frequencies around the Cutoff frequency. In some filters, when this control is turned up the filter goes into self oscillation producing a sine wave.

Usually there is a fixed slope set on the filter described in dB per octave. The higher this value, the more severely the frequencies above the Cutoff point are attenuated or reduced. Typical filters are set to 12, 18 or 24 dB/octave. These different values have different sounds.

Filters can exist in several forms.

- Low pass filters – the most common type. They filter out all the frequencies above the Cutoff value. The more you increase the value of the Cutoff the more the higher frequencies are let through.

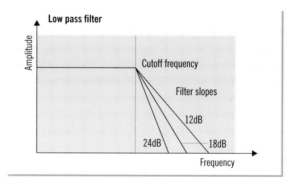

- High pass filter – could be seen as the opposite of the Low Pass filter. Turning up the Cutoff attenuates the low frequencies.

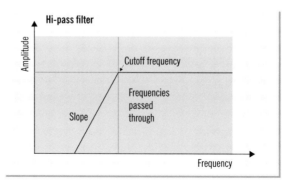

- Band pass filter – allows a range of frequencies around the Cutoff to pass while rejecting both upper and lower frequencies.
- Band reject filter – the opposite of the band pass filter. Upper and lower frequencies are let through while those around the Cutoff are attenuated.

Some filters can distort at extreme setting producing 'fat' or 'warm' tones. Filters are probably the main reason for the 'sound' of a given synthesiser.

Envelope generators (ADSR or EG)

The sound of the filtered oscillators can be modified using envelope generators. The envelope of the sound describes the following parameters – though some synthesisers have more.

- Attack – sets the speed at which the sound starts. A fast attack time means the notes start immediately .
- Decay – sets the speed at which the note falls to the sustain level.
- Sustain – sets the level of the sound plays at while a key is pressed.
- Release – sets the speed at which the note decays after a key is released.

These values can often be modified by how hard a key is struck or how far up a keyboard a note is. Envelope generators can also be used to modify the Filter Cutoff to produce filter sweeps.

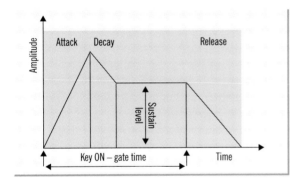

Amplifier (VCA)

This sets the level of the final sound after it's been through all the parts of the synthesiser. This is the part that's modulated by the EG when it's controlling amplitude.

Low Frequency Oscillator (LFO)

Synthesisers can be modulated using Low Frequency Oscillators. These are similar to the audio oscillators described above, but their output is used to modulate the other sections of the synthesiser. LFOs often have various waveforms producing different effects.

- If LFOs are applied to oscillators, the effect is one of vibrato or pitch modulation.
- If LFOs are applied to the pulse width of a square wave, pulse width modulation (PWM) occurs sweeping between the 'thin' and 'nasal' oscillator sound.

- If LFOs are applied to the Amplifier, the effect is one of tremolo or amplitude modulation.
- If LFOs are applied to the Filter, the effect is one of 'wah'

These actual effects depend on the type of waveform produced by the LFOs:

- Sine wave – produces a smooth vibrato or tremolo.
- Triangle or sawtooth wave – produces a more pronounced vibrato or tremolo or wah effect.
- Random – generates a less predictable modulation of the VCO, VCA or VCF. Useful if you want to add 'movement' to a sounds.

Some 'analogue style' synthesisers may have more or less of these features, but they are the basic building blocks of synthesis and of Logics Virtual synthesisers.

Other synthesis types

FM

FM synthesis or Frequency modulation is based on the modulation of one oscillator's frequency with another. Some of Logics instruments offer a simple FM generator.

In these cases, a simple sine wave generated by one oscillator (the carrier) is modulated by the frequency of another oscillator (the modulator). The modulator could be a sine wave, but other waveforms can produce interesting tones too. Both the modulator and carrier produce signals in the audible spectrum. It's similar to a LFO modulating the pitch of the oscillator to produce vibrato – however the LFO produces low frequency, non-audible waveforms.

As you change the frequency of the modulator, the harmonic content of the carrier changes. If you use a LFO, Envelope generator or other modulation source to change this frequency, the carrier will sweep through different harmonics – similar to a ADSR sweep of the Filter Cutoff frequency. If the frequency deviation ratio of the modulator to carrier is an integer, harmonic waveforms are generated. If it's not, inharmonic tones are produced.

Digital synthesis

Digital synthesisers usually have digital recreations of the usual analogue waveforms alongside other, digitally generated, ones. These could be samples of real audio recordings or completely new, unusual, waveforms. They can have digital or analogue filters, often with more parameters and control than their analogue counterparts. They often have several Envelope generators too and built-in digital effects.

Additionally, you may be able to sweep through the different digital waveforms (wavetable synthesis) or change the oscillator mix in real time (vector synthesis).

The free Virtual Instruments

Emagic Logic comes with three free Virtual instruments. These are:

The ESM Virtual Monophonic Synthesiser

This is designed for bass sounds but is entirely capable of lead lines too. It has a monophonic audio output and can play one note at a time.

The ESE Virtual Ensemble Synthesiser

This is an 8 voice polyphonic Virtual Synthesiser designed for pad sounds. It has a stereo audio output. Use this for cheesy pads or where you don't want too fat a sound.

The ESP Virtual Polyphonic Synthesiser

This is an 8 voice polyphonic Virtual Synthesiser designed for brass, strings and other typical polysynth sounds. It has a stereo audio output. This is the classic '80s 'low cost synth' emulation.

All three synths are great for dance music – but you can use them in many other types of music with great results.

All the synths have once oscillator per voice and simple interfaces. But don't let this put you off – you can add as many of these to a song as your CPU will allow – and they are very CPU-lite. You can process them with all of Logic Audio's plug-in effects .You can use these Virtual Instruments to produce some great sounds. It's also worthwhile experimenting with these synthesisers – their parameters have many similarities with other Virtual Instruments.

Some background

These synthesisers, and many other Virtual Instruments, are based on the principle of analogue subtractive synthesis. In this form of synthesis, the tone is produced by oscillators (OSC). The output from these are then processed by filters (VCF) which change the tone of the oscillator sound. The level of the oscillator and Cutoff frequency of the Filter can be modified over time using envelope generators (ADSR). An amplifier connects the electronics to the outside world (VCA). You can use Low Frequency Oscillators (LFO) to modulate the pitch of the oscillators (vibrato), the filter (wah) and the amplifier (tremolo). The sound may be passed through a chorus or ensemble effect to fatten up the sound. Finally, there's a volume control to set the overall level of the instrument.

The ESM Virtual Monophonic Synthesiser

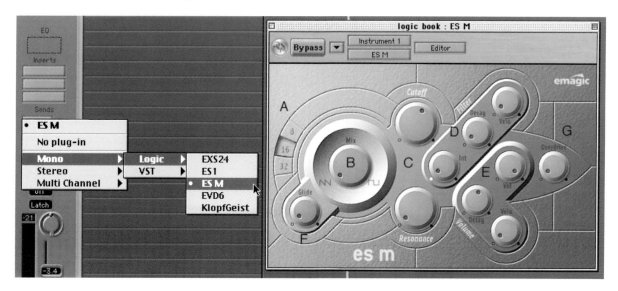

The ESM is a good start for getting the feel of Logic's Virtual Instruments. Try selecting some of the sounds from the pull down menu or using the Key commands to change presets. See how the settings change from preset to preset.

Figure 6.1
The ESM Virtual Monophonic Synthesiser

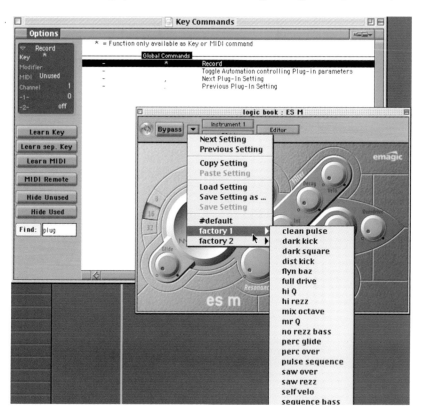

Figure 6.2

Here's how the various parts change the sounds.

A   Footage. This determines the pitch of the sound in octave steps, 8 being the highest pitch and 32 the lowest. The numbers are leftovers from how the pitch of organ pipes were described in feet.

B   This determines the shape of the waveform output by the oscillator. The ESM has one oscillator. If you turn the control to the left the waveform is a sawtooth wave. Fully to the right it outputs a square wave. If you put the control in between you get a mixed waveform.

C   This is the filter. The top control sets the Cutoff frequency of the filter. Turn the knob fully to the left to make the sound duller, to the right to make it brighter. The bottom control is the Resonance control. If you turn this to the right you will hear the tone change. The ESM filter has a fixed slope of 24dB per octave. It's a 'warm' filter! The filter on the ESM can be made to self oscillate. If you turn the Resonance fully to the right and adjust the Cutoff frequency, you'll hear a high frequency pure sine-like tone.

D   This is the envelope generator for the filter. With this you can modulate the Cutoff frequency over time. You us use this to open and close the filter cutoff when you press a key. INT sets the intensity of this modulation – this control has to be turned to the right for the following controls to work. Decay sets the speed that the filter cutoff closes. Velo makes the filter envelope velocity sensitive so the harder you hit a key, the greater the effect.

E   This is the envelope generator for the amplifier. You can make the volume of the synth change over time. The Decay control sets how quickly the volume of the sound falls to silence. Velo sets the velocity sensitivity of the sound, so the harder you hit a key, the louder the sound. Vol sets the overall level of the sound.

F   If you turn the Glide control to the right and play a new note without releasing the previous note, the sound sweeps up in pitch to the next note. If you play and release the previous note before playing another, no Glide is heard.

G   Overdrive is a kind of distortion effect. It increases the harmonic content of the sound – and the level.

Saving sounds

You can load a sound, modify it and save it under another name using the menu on the plug-in.

Figure 6.3

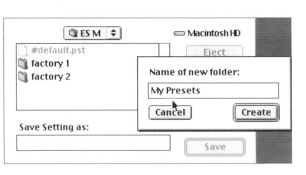

Tip

Use the square wave for flute like and rounded tones. The triangle wave is harsher with more harmonics.

Tip

The ESM is really useful for dance music bass sounds

Tip

Save your sounds in the ESM folder in the Logic Audio folder. You can create subfolders within this folder and store your sounds there.

The ESM produces a single output monophonic sound. Any Instrument audio object you insert it on will be mono.

Figure 6.4

The ESE Virtual Ensemble Synthesiser

Figure 6.5
The ESE Virtual Ensemble Synthesiser

You select and save sounds on the ESE in exactly the same way as the ESM. The ESE however is a stereo instrument and the Instrument audio object it's inserted in will be a stereo one.

Figure 6.6
The ESE is a stereo instrument and the Instrument audio object it's inserted in will be a stereo one.

Tip

Use the chorus and Ensemble in alongside small amount of vibrato or pulse width modulation to fatten up the sound.

You'll notice many similarities to the ESM.

A The overall pitch of the ESP in octave steps. Note that the ESM doesn't go as low as the ESM – the range is 4 to 16 feet
B The leftmost setting of the Wave control outputs a sawtooth wave. Turning the knob from the oscillator outputs a square wave. As you sweep across the square wave the pulse width changes, as shown below.

C When the Wave control is set to Sawtooth, this knob defines the amount of vibrato – the oscillator is frequency modulated. When the oscillator is outputting a square wave, the pulse width is swept or modulated. This is called 'Pulse width Modulation' or PWM. Both these parameters can add 'movement' to a static oscillator sound.
D The Speed control sets the speed of the sweep or the vibrato.
E The filter is exactly the same as for the ESM
F The Attack and Release times (how long the note takes to start and how long it takes to decay to silence after the key is released).are set here.
G The AR int knob sets the amount that the Filter is affected by the Attack and Release controls. At a value of 0, only the volume is affected by the Attack and Release. As you turn this value up, the Cutoff frequency of the filter is also affected. Setting it to negative values makes the Attack and Release controls work the opposite way on the Filter alone.
    For example, if you set a slow Attack and Release (volume swells in and then decays slowly), setting the AR int control to a negative value makes the filter Cutoff increase in intensity and decrease rapidly. At extreme settings you may not notice this effect – the volume envelope has priority.
H The Velo Filter control sets the amount by which the Filter Cutoff control is modulated by the incoming velocity of the MIDI controller keyboard. Harder key hits increase the Cutoff frequency.
I The Velo Volume defines the velocity sensitivity of the sound. If it's full to the left there is no velocity sensitivity.
J The Volume control sets the master volume of the ESE.
K There are three different chorus settings for 'fattening up' the sound. These make the ESE sounds more lush and expansive. They can all be turned off.

The ESP Virtual Polyphonic Synthesiser

Again the ESP has many similarities to the ESM and ESE.

A Selects the overall pitch in octave steps.
B On the ESP, several waveforms can be mixed together to increase the complexity of the sound. The fader on the right generates noise for wind and surf effects or adding 'grunge' to the sound. The three square waves are at different pitches for adding extra depth to the sound – these are called sub oscillators.
C Moving this knob towards Vib adds vibrato to the oscillators. Moving it to the right modulates the filter cut off for wah effects. Exactly what the wah effect sounds like depends upon the filter settings.
D The speed control sets the rate of two parameters above – i.e. the speed of the vibrato and the rate of the wah.

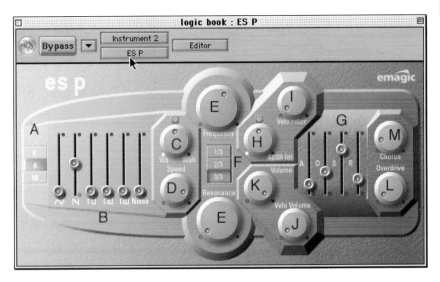

Figure 6.7
The ESP Virtual Polyphonic Synthesiser

E   The filter is identical to the ESE and ESM
F   These values set the 'Keyboard follow' of the sound. When set to 3/3, the filter
    behaves the same irrespective of what note you play on a keyboard. Setting it
    to 1/3 means the sound gets duller as you play higher up the keyboard. The
    parameters effectively set the filter Cutoff by MIDI note number.
G   The ADSR sets the Attack, Decay, Sustain and Release of the sound. This
    affects the volume of the sound.
H   Turning this clockwise sends the filter Cutoff through the ADSR. Using this you
    can open and close the filter using the settings. Negative values make the filter
    modulation behave in the opposite way to the volume – just as in the ESE.
I   The Velo filter sets the amount by which the filter Cutoff frequency is modulated
    by the velocity of the keyboard. Setting this to a high value means that the
    harder you hit the key, the brighter the sound.
J   The Velo volume sets the velocity sensitivity of the sound. High values mean
    that the sound becomes more velocity sensitive.
K   This sets the overall volume of the sound.
L   Overdrive adds distortion to the sound – this generates extra harmonics.
M   Turn the knob to the right to add a chorus effect to fatten up the sound.

Tip

The best way to create new sounds is to select a preset sound that is similar to the one you are aiming for. Then you can adjust the controls to make the sound closer to the one you want.

The ES1 Synthesiser

The ES1 is a virtual analogue synthesiser similar to the ESM that comes free with Logic. It looks a little more complex and has more parameters than the ESM, but the basic layout is the same. A single oscillator feeds through a filter into an ADSR and amplifier, like the ESM. But there are more filter types, more modulation possibilities and more oscillator parameters. The ES1 can also play polyphonically – i.e. more than one note at a time. The ES1 can be instanced either in Mono mode, in which it plays through only one output, or Stereo. In this case the Chorus effects are in Stereo.

Figure 7.1
The ES1 Synthesiser

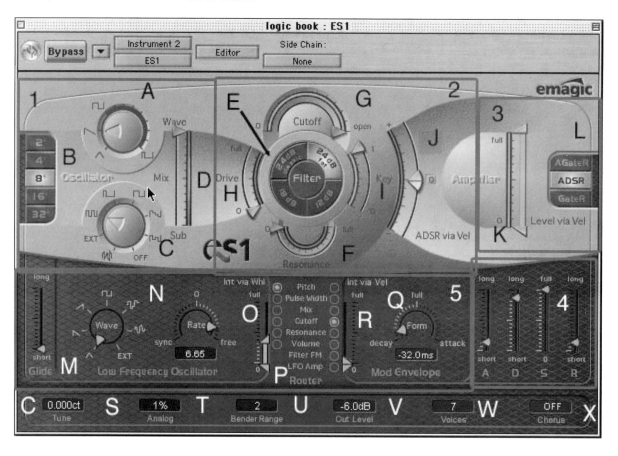

The first thing to do with the ES1 is listen to some of the presets that come with it. These will give you a 'range' of sounds the ES1 excels at.

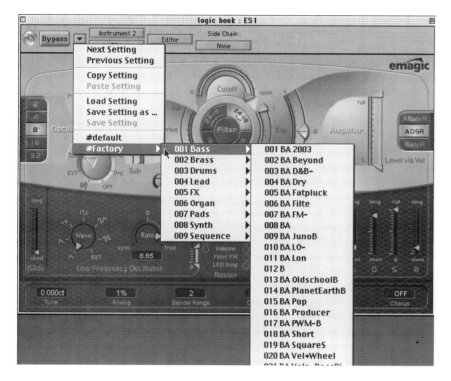

Figure 7.2
Listen to the presets.

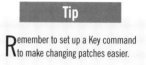

Tip

Remember to set up a Key command to make changing patches easier.

Info

The ES1 might be best for bass, lead, and effects – but don't dismiss its possibilities for producing pad and atmospheric-like sounds. The ADSR on the ES1 has a very fast attack – making it ideal for percussive sounds too.

Figure 7.1 shows the different sections of the ES1

Section 1 – the sound sources

The single oscillator can provide a sine, sawtooth and square wave (A). The pulse width of the square wave can be varied manually (the blue line around the knob between the positions shown on the right. The pulse width can also be modulated – see the section on modulation described below. The octave is chosen at (B) – the smaller the number, the higher the pitch. There is also a sub-oscillator that can be mixed in to add a waveform at one and two octaves below the main oscillator (C). This Sub oscillator can have several different waveforms, selected by the knob and can also act as a noise generator (pictured right). The Mix slider (D) is used to blend the level of the main oscillator and the sub. If the slider is fully up you just hear the main oscillator; fully down and you just hear the sub.

Section 2 – the filters

The ES1 contains three different filter types, each with different slopes – 12, 18 and 24 dB per octave (E). In addition, the 24dB filter comes in two types – 'Classic' and 'Fat'. The latter filter compensates for the loss in low frequencies as the Resonance control is turned up. There are the standard Resonance (F) and Cutoff controls (G) and the filters can be coaxed into self oscillation with the Resonance

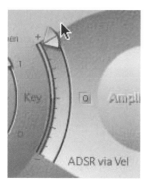

Figure 7.3
The ADSR via Vel control

Figure 7.4 (left)
The Level via Vel control

Figure 7.5 (right)
The blue line in between the knobs is effectively the velocity range.

control turned fully on. The Drive control overloads the filter for a 'fat' and 'richer' filter sound (H). Turning up the Key slider (I) makes the Cutoff frequency follow the MIDI note number. If it's set to 0, playing higher notes will sound progressively duller, mimicking a 'real' instrument. Turning the control up makes the relationship more constant, so that at setting 1, the sound is the same across the note range. The ADSR via Vel control (J) sets the intensity at which the filter is sent to the ADSR. You'll notice that there are two triangular knobs. These affect the way in which the filter is sent to the ADSR depending on the velocity of the incoming MIDI data. The control can be set to send a positive value to the ADSR or a negative value – in which case a slow Attack set on the ADSR will become a fast attack of the filter.

Here's how the Velocity control works. If both knobs are close together there is no difference in the amount of the filter sent to the ADSR whatever the velocity. This mimics 'classic' non-velocity sensitive synthesisers. If you then push both to 1 this sends the whole filter output to the ADSR for classic filter sweeps.

If you separate the knobs, the lower one is the setting to send the filter to the ADSR at MIDI velocity =1, and the upper at velocity = 127. How far apart the knobs are defines the velocity range. So the quieter you hit a key, the less the fil-ter output is sent to the ADSR (or a negative value is sent) and the harder you hit the key, the more filter output is sent, making the filter of the ES1 highly respon-sive to MIDI note velocity.

Section 3 – the Amplifier

The Level via Vel control (K) sets the output of the ES1. You'll notice that there are two triangular knobs (Figure 7.4). If these are placed together and moved togeth-er, the ES1 does not respond to incoming velocity and the volume is the same no matter how hard you hit a key, the maximum value being set by the control.

If you separate the controls, the upper knob sets the maximum MIDI velocity value and the lower the minimum, making the ES1 velocity sensitive. The blue line in between the knobs is effectively the velocity range.

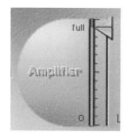 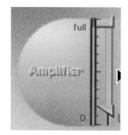

The remaining Amplifier controls (L) defines which ADSR controls have an effect on the amplifier.

• AgateR sends the amplifier through Attack and Release setting in the ADSR, ignoring the Decay and Sustain settings. This means that, after the Attack, the level remains the same as long as a key is pressed. When the key is released, the Amplifier follows the Release setting.

- ADSR sends the amplifier through all ADSR settings.
- GaterR sets the Attack time to zero, ignores the Decay and Sustain settings, and only uses the release setting when the key is released.

Section 4 – the ADSR

The ADSR (Attack, Decay, sustain and Release) acts on both the Amplifier and Filter as seen above, although the way in which the filter can be routed through the ADSR can be varied.

Section 5 – the modulators

The Glide control (M) sets the time a note takes to slide up in pitch to another note. It's behaviour is defined by the number of voices assigned.

The Low Frequency Oscillator (LFO) (N) is used to modulate various parts of the ES1 as defined by the Router described below. There are different waveforms as well as an EXT setting that uses an external Side chain signal, such as a audio track, as a modulation source. Turning the Rate knob from 0 to Free sets a frequency for the LFO to work at. Turning the knob from 0 to sync, makes the LFO frequency dependant and in time with the track.

The Int Via Wheel control (O) defines the range of the Modulation Wheel when used to control the LFO. If the two controls are set together, this sets LFO Modulation without the wheel being used. If you split them the lower knob gives the lower setting of the Wheel, the upper knob the maximum.

The distance between the knobs sets the maximum and minimum modulation from the wheel.

The left side of the Router (P) defines which section of the ES1 is modulated by the LFO. The options are;

Figure 7.6
Modulation set by wheel

- Pitch – the LFO modulates the pitch of the oscillators – vibrato.
- Pulse width – the LFO modulates the pulse width of the square wave if that is chosen in the Oscillator – pulse width modulation.
- Mix – the LFO modulates the MIX control that blends the Oscillator and the Sub.
- Cutoff – the LFO modulates the filter Cutoff – Wah.
- Resonance – the LFO modulates the filter Resonance.
- Volume – the LFO modulates the Amplifier volume – Tremolo.

The Mod Envelope (Q) sets the way the LFO modulation fades in and out. It can be set to a percussive type setting (Decay) or slower attack type settings. It works in conjunction with the right side of the Router (P). Setting it to Full sends the Modulation envelope through the ADSR.

The Router has two extra settings when using the Mod Envelope:

Figure 7.7
Modulation set to work without wheel

- Filter FM – if the filter is in self oscillation mode, metallic, bell-like tones can be created. Otherwise, musically useful distortion occurs.
- LFO amp – Setting an Attack setting in the Mod envelope will produce delayed LFO modulation – i.e. the modulation occurs some time after a key is pressed.

The Int via Vel control(R) controls the velocity sensitivity of the Mod Envelope. The upper control sets the intensity at maximum MIDI velocity, the lower at the minimum. Placing the two controls together sets a fixed mod envelope intensity unaffected by velocity. See the Int via Whl control (O).

Section 6 – various controls

- Tune (S) – sets the overall tuning of the ES1.
- Analogue (T) – varies the pitch of each note to emulate analogy synthesiser tuning instabilities. The ES1 will sound out of tune at high settings!
- Bender range (U) – sets the range of the pitch bender wheel on your MIDI controller in semitones.
- Out Level (V) – sets the master volume of the ES1.
- Voices (W) – sets the number of voices (simultaneous notes) played by the ES1. The more voices used, the higher the CPU burden.

The setting 'Legato' means that if you play another note before releasing the previous one (Legato playing style), the ADSR will not be triggered, but the Glide will if set to a value above zero. Playing staccato (releasing a key before another is played) will allow the ADSR to trigger and the Glide to be turned off. Legato is a monophonic mode (one voice only) and is useful for expressive lead line playing.

- Chorus (X) – adds a chorus or ensemble effect to 'fatten' up the ES1, giving the impression it has several oscillators per voice.

Making sounds

That's covered the basics – but how do we create sounds using the ES1? It's useful to have a 'reset' patch that allows us to hear the effects of the different parts of the synthesiser clearly. A reset patch is shown in Figure 7.8. Always reload this when you want to explore the ES1's controls.

Figure 7.8
Reset patch

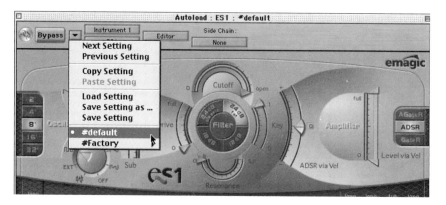

Try the following and listen to the results.

- Try changing the Wave to hear the different Timbres the ES1 has to offer.
- Try pulling the Mix slider to Sub to hear the Sub's waveforms.
- Try selecting the different filters and moving the Cutoff and Resonance to hear the differences.

- Try changing the ADSR values. Turn the Attack slider up to create a level rise when you play a key. Try turning both the ADSR via vel knobs up to create a filter swell.
- Try adding LFO waveform and rate. Also try different Routings for the LFO.
- Try the Analogue settings.
- Try the Chorus settings.

These should give you a feel for the ES1 controls. When you understand what a control does, you can load other presets and see what is making what contribution to the sound.

Info

With some parameters on the ES1 you may have to re-hit a key to hear the changes.

Tip

Load a preset, modify it to your hearts content then re-save under a new name in a new folder. It's easy to build up a library of your own sounds.

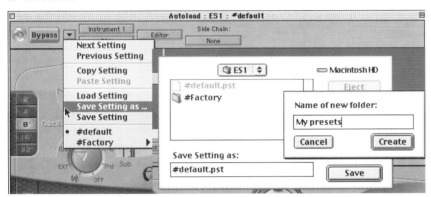

Here's a rundown on some of the presets.

Bass sound – Preset:Ba basic

Figure 7.9
Bass sound presets.

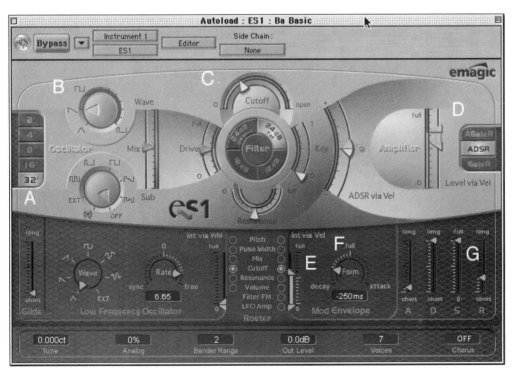

This sound should be played at the lower end of the keyboard. The main parameters defining this sound are as follows.

- Main oscillator at 32' (A) – This is a low octave setting.
- Main oscillator wave set to sawtooth (B) – this gives a sound rich in harmonics.
- Filter Cutoff and Resonance set to make a warm, round tone (C).
- Amplifier set to give a slight velocity sensitivity (D).
- Int via Vel set to Filter Cutoff to create some tonal movement when played via a velocity sensitive keyboard (E).
- Mod Envelope set towards decay as it's a percussive tone(F).
- ADSR set to a rapid attack, quick decay, long sustain and rapid release of the note when the key is released (G).

Modifications to the preset
Try modifying the sound as follows

- Add a Sub tone to make the sound even bassier (Figure 7.10).
- Change the Cutoff and Resonance to change the tonal characteristic of the sound (Figure 7.11).

Figure 7.10 (Left)
Add a Sub tone

Figure 7.11 (right)
Change the Cutoff and Resonance

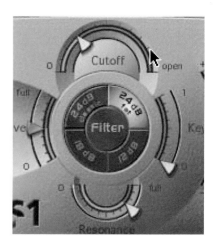

- Enable the modulation control of the LFO to add movement to the sound using the Modulation Wheel on your MIDI controller. Set the Router to pitch for vibrato or the Cutoff for wah.

Figure 7.12
Enable the modulation control of the LFO

Figure 7.13
Change the Voices parameter to 'legato'

- Change the Voices parameter to 'legato' to add expressiveness to playing. This makes the sound monophonic – perfect for a bass sound.

Lead sound – Ld Moog Classic 2

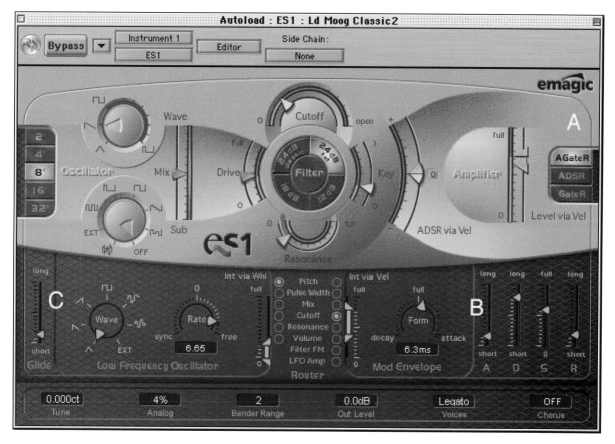

Figure 7.14
Ld Moog Classic 2

Play this sound at the upper end of the keyboard and use the pitch bend and modulation wheel.

The main parameters that make up this sound are:

- Main Oscillator set to a sawtooth wave for a sound rich in harmonics and the 8' setting gives a higher octave pitch than the bass sound described earlier.
- Filter set to 24dB 'fat' for a rich sound that maintains its bass content whatever the settings of the filter. Resonance and Cutoff set to low values to mute the harmonics for a round tone.
- Drive set to produce a cutting filter sound.
- Key set so that the sound gets less bright as you play up the keyboard.
- Small amounts of vibrato controllable via the modulation wheel.
- Amplifier set to just the Attack and Release sections of the ADSR allowing the D and S values to affect only the filter (A).
- Voices set to Legato so that ADSR only affects the sound when a key is released when a new one is played. It also makes the sound monophonic which is perfect for a lead sound.
- Slight slow Attack to make the sound less percussive (B).
- Slight Glide setting that will only be heard when the sound is played in a Legato style. Releasing each key stops the Glide affecting the sound.

> **Tip**
>
> Lead sounds can often be really useful as bass sounds when transposed down. The reverse is also true!

Modifications to the sound

- Change the Resonance and Cutoff settings.
- Choose a different LFO wave and try modulating other sources using the Router.
- Select a different filter type.
- Change the ADSR and Level via vel settings to increase velocity sensitivity.
- Turn up the Drive control to make the sound bite more.

Pad sound – 045 Synth Pad 3

This sound can be played all over the keyboard. Play with less notes at the lower end to reduce muddiness.

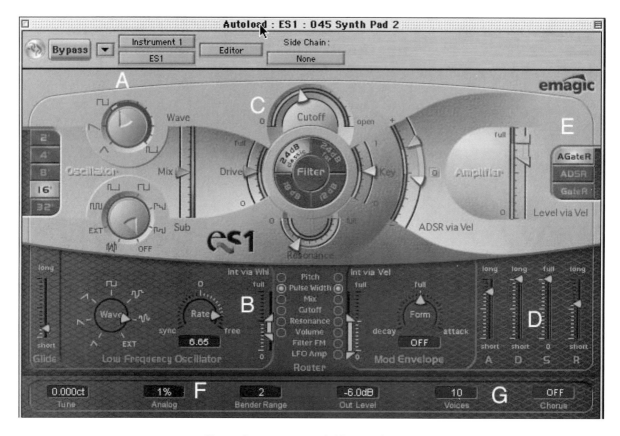

Figure 7.15
045 Synth Pad 3

The main parameters of this sound are:

- Main Oscillator waveform set to a Square wave (A). The wave's pulse width is modulated by the LFO, the intensity of which can be changed using the Modulation wheel (B). The LFO sine wave makes it a regular smooth modulation.
- Filter set to 24dB 'Classic' for a thinner sound across the keyboard (C). the Cutoff and Resonance is set for a mellow tone.
- ADSR set to a slow attack and long release (D).

- Amplifier set to AgateR to let the S and R parameters to be used by the filter only (E).
- Analogue parameter set to emulate the drift of oscillators – this adds to the sounds perceived 'warmth' (F).
- Voices set to 10 for full polyphonic playing (G).

Sound effect – Wind – Efx

This sound emulates the sound of wind blowing. Play on any key – it's an un-pitched sound.

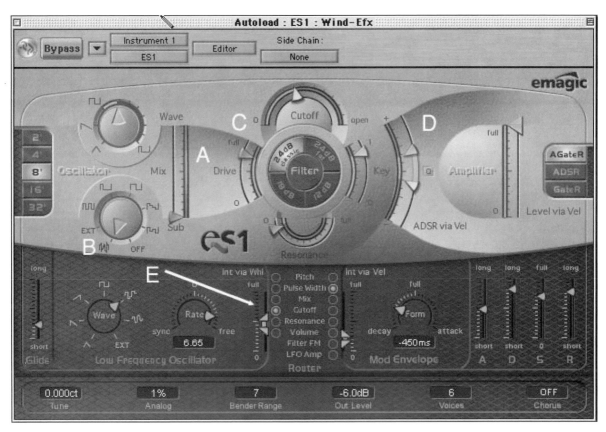

Figure 7.16
Sound effect – Wind – Efx

The main parameters of this sound are as follows;

- Mix slider set to Sub – the main oscillator is turned off (A).
- The sub waveform is set to Noise (B).
- Drive control is set to a high position to add bite (C).
- ADSR via Vel is set for some velocity control to add variation (D).
- LFO wave set to random to simulate the unpredictable nature of wind noise. The LFO is set to drive the Cutoff via the Router to create blowing noises by modulating the filter (E).

Modifications to the sound

Try varying the Cutoff and Resonance controls to vary the tone of the wind.

Percussive sound – E-kick

This simulates the electronic bass drum of analogue drum machines. Played at the low end it's a bass drum. Played at the high end it's an electronic tomtom!

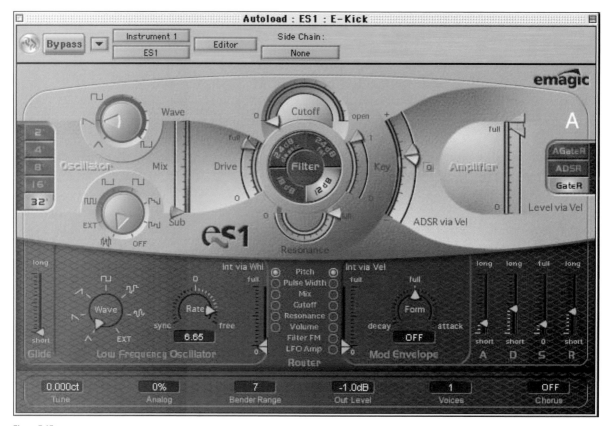

Figure 7.17
Percussive sound – E-kick

Figure 7.18
Mixing in the Oscillator

The main parameters of this sound are as follows:

- The Mix slider is set fully down so only the Sub waveform is heard. The Sub waveform is set to noise.
- Drive is full on to add bite.
- A 12 dB filter for a deeper sound. Resonance is set to full and the Cutoff to zero, pushing the filter into self oscillation generating the round tone that is the body of the sound. The Key parameter is set to 1, opening the Filter at high MIDI note values, i.e. higher up the keyboard.
- The GateR is set to on, allowing the ADS part of the ADSR to be bypassed. This creates a fast percussive sound as if the Attack parameter was set to a short value. The filter now uses the ADSR only – note the slow attack of the filter (A)

Modifications to the sound
- Try changing the filter parameters to produce other percussion sounds.
- Try changing the D control on the ADSR to tighten up the filter opening and closing.
- Try mixing in the Oscillator to add pitched tones.

The ES2 Synthesiser

The ES2 is a sophisticated polyphonic synthesiser. It models several popular types of synthesis. However, many of the concepts it uses are similar to those in the free ESM, ESE and ESP synthesisers described in Chapter 6

Before you get to grips with programming the ES2, check out some of the many presets supplied with the synthesiser.

Figure 8.1
Some of the ES2 Synthesiser presets

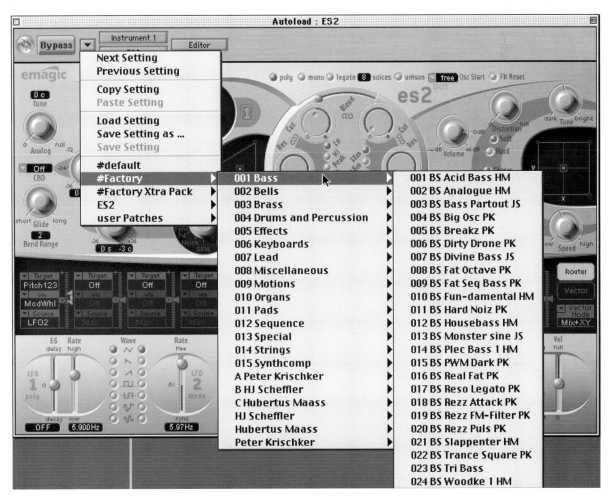

The ES2 models the following types of synthesis:

Analogue synthesiser

The ES2 is a 3 oscillator virtual analogue synthesiser, with classic filters and modulation sources. Real life hardware examples are the Sequential Circuits Prophet 5 and Roland Jupiter series.

Digital synthesiser

The oscillators can generate many more waveforms than the 'traditional' Sine, Square or Triangle allowing the ES2 many more timbral possibilities. Examples are the Ensoniq SQ1 and Roland D50 synthesisers.

Wave sequencing synthesiser

You can dynamically cross fade between these digital waves as a note is held down (using the 'Triangle'), allowing the sound to radically change over time. Real life examples are the Waldorf Wave, Sequential Circuits VS and the Korg Wavestation.

However, the filters and modulation controls on the ES2 are far more advanced than on their hardware counterparts allowing some truly unique sounds to be produced as well as emulations of traditional machines.

At first glance the ES2 looks a complex beast. However if we break it down into sections it should look more manageable and bear relationships to what we've learned in previous chapters.

- Section 1 – the Oscillators. The ES2 has 3.
- Section 2 – the Keyboard mode.
- Section 3 – the Filters. The ES2 has 2.
- Section 4 – the output stage. This incorporates the volume control, Chorus, a Sine wave, Distortion with associated tone control.
- Section 5 – LFO section. The ES2 has two Low Frequency Oscillators.
- Section 6 – ADSR section. The ES2 has two flexible ADSRs and a AD section.
- Section 7 – the Router. The ES2 has a flexible modulation routing section.
- Section 8 – the Square, Triangle and Vector mode.
- Section 9 – the Random sound generator.

As you can see the ES2 is a sort of 'super' ES1 – as its name implies!

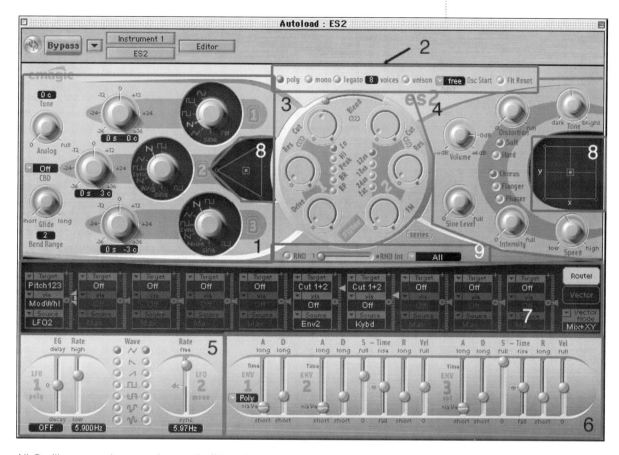

All Oscillators can be turned on and off by clicking on the number next to the oscillator.

Figure 8.2
The ES2 Synthesiser

Figure 8.3
Oscillator on

Figure 8.4
Oscillator off

Section 1 – the oscillators

The three oscillators on the ES2 are similar to each other, but have some differences.

Oscillator 1

This has proper sine wave (A), two types of square wave with different pulse widths (B), triangle (C) and sawtooth (D) (Figure 8.5).

There is also a 'sine' setting (Figure 8.6). If you hold down the mouse key over this and drag up and down you'll see the Digiwaves. These are 100 digitally stored waveforms that significantly expand the tonal palate of the ES2.

Figure 8.5
Oscillator 1

Tip

When experimenting with oscillator tones and mixes, load the 'Reset' patch.

Figure 8.6

Dragging the mouse between the sine icon and the FM setting – this can be used for frequency modulation in a similar way to the Yamaha DX7 (Figure 8.7).

Figure 8.7
Dragging the mouse between the sine icon and the FM setting

Figure 8.8
The pitch of the oscillator is set using the knob to the left of the waveform selector. For fine control you can click drag the mouse over the numbers.

Figure 8.9
Oscillator 2

Figure 8.10
Oscillator 3

Oscillator 2

This has a sawtooth wave, triangle wave, a square and triangle wave that can be synchronised to oscillator 1 (A), a ring modulator (B), the Digiwaves (C) and a square wave that has a variable pulse width (D).

Oscillator 3

This has a sawtooth wave, triangle wave, a square and triangle wave that can be synchronised to oscillator 1 (A), coloured noise (B), the Digiwaves (C) and a square wave that has a variable pulse width (D).

Other oscillator parameters

Tune (Figure 8.11)

This sets the overall pitch of the ES2 in cents. There are 100 cents to a semitone.

Analogue (Figure 8.12)

This control varies the pitch and the Cutoff frequency of the ES2 in an attempt to emulate the instability of hardware analogue synthesisers. If the ES2 is in Unison mode, analogue affects the detuning of the oscillators. If the Voices parameter is set to 1 and Legato is OFF, the analogue parameter has no effect.

Figures 8.11 and 8.12

CBD (Constant Beat Detuning) (Figure 8.13)

When the Oscillators are detuned with respect to each other, you'll get a 'beating' effect which can add to the richness of a sound. Unfortunately, you can have a situation where at higher pitches, the beating just sounds out of tune. CBD attempts to solve this problem. It's best to try one of the values of CBD and play both high and low notes to see if it's the effect you want.

Glide (Figure 8.14)

This parameter sets the time it takes for one note to slide up to another. If the ES2 is set to legato, the Glide is only heard if you keep a previous key down while playing another – like the ES1.

Bend range (Figure 8.15)

Sets the bend range for the Pitch controller on your MIDI keyboard, or other controller, in semitones.

Figures 8.13, 8.14 and 8.15

Section 2 – the keyboard mode

These controls set the way in which the ES2 responds to playing.

- Poly – allows you to play as many voices as is set in the Voices parameter.
- Mono – allows only one note at a time to be played. In this mode the Glide and Filter envelope re-trigger whenever you press a new key.
- Legato – like mono, in that only one note at time can be played. However the Glide and Filter envelope only re-trigger when you release the last key before pressing another, allowing more expressive playing.
- Voices – the number of simultaneous voices that the ES2 can play.
- Unison – this stacks all the voices set in the Voices parameter onto a single note, creating a really fat sound! The way it works depends on the setting of the following.
- Unison with mono or legato set – this stacks all the voices set in the Voices parameter to one note. I.e. if you have Voices set to 4, when you play a note it will play all 4 voices at once. If you're using 3 oscillators per voice, each note will sound 16 oscillators!
- Unison with poly set – this allows polyphonic playing with but with voices stacked as described above. If you have Voices set to 4 with these parameters set, each note will play 2 voices and the polyphony will be halved to 2 notes at a time.

Osc start

As oscillators produce sound using periodic waveforms, when you press a key, you're never sure at what part of the waveform the sound will start at. You can force the ES2 to start the waveform of the oscillators either at the zero crossing point (the 'soft' parameter) or the highest point of the waveform (the 'hard' parameter).
    Soundwise, the effects of the Osc start values is as follows:

- Free – mimics the oscillators of an analogue synthesiser – a warm sound.
- Soft – mimics the oscillators of a digital synthesiser – a harder sound.
- Hard – makes the start of each note more 'punchy' if the Attack part of the ADSR controlling the volume is set to 'short'.

Flt reset

When the filter is set to self oscillation, turn this parameter on to make sure the filter re-triggers when a note is played, allowing you to hear the self-triggered sinewave.

The Triangle

Figure 8.16
The Triangle

This is a kind of 'virtual' joystick. Dragging the button (A) varies the level of the oscillators and thus the mix between them. As this movement is easily automated, it can be used to emulate the vector joystick of synthesisers such as the Korg Wavestation or Sequential Circuits Prophet VS.

Section 3 – the filters

The ES2 has two filters that can be set to several filter types and can be used in series or parallel. The type is selected by the button at A (right).

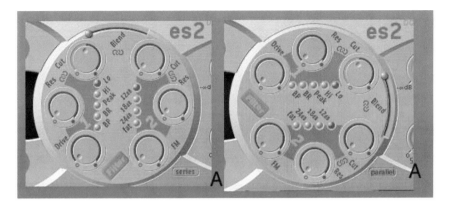

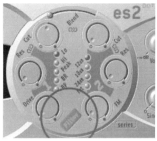

Figure 8.17
ES2 has two filters

- Filter in series – the signal passes through the first filter then the second filter – if the Filter bend parameter is set to zero. The output is in mono and can be panned left or right (pic above left).
- Filter in parallel – the oscillator signal passes through both the filters simultaneously when filter blend is set to zero. The two outputs can then be panned in stereo for different filter processing in each channel (pic above right).

You can just use one filter by dragging the filter blend control toward that filter (Figure 8.19). You can also cross fade the filters by modulating the blend control in the Router.

The drive control affects the sound in various ways depending on the setting on the filter.

In parallel mode, the drive affects both filters equally (Figure 8.20).

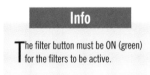

> **Info**
>
> The filter button must be ON (green) for the filters to be active.

Figure 8.19
Dragging the filter blend control.

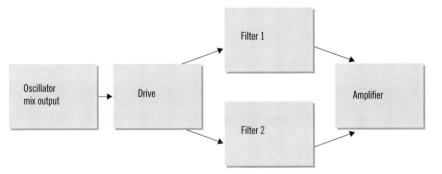

Figure 8.20

In serial mode, it depends on the setting of the Filter blend control (Figure 8.21)

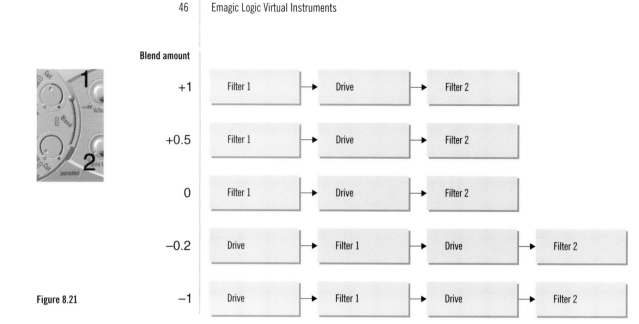

Blend amount

Figure 8.21

The two filters are different. Filter 1 can be used in the following modes.

- Lo – a 24dB per octave low pass filter.
- Hi – a hi pass filter.
- Peak – a peak filter.
- BP – a band pass filter.
- BR – a band reject filter.

Filter 2 is a low pass filter that can be used with the following slopes

- 12, 18 and 24 dB per octave.

The Fat setting replaces low frequencies lost as the Resonance value is increased.

The chain symbol
The chain symbol (left) allows simultaneous use of the Cutoff and Resonance controls of the filter chosen.

- Clicking and holding the mouse and moving it up and down over the chain symbol modifies the Cutoff.
- Clicking and holding the mouse and moving it side to side over the chain symbol modifies the Resonance.
- Clicking and holding the mouse over the chain symbol and moving diagonally modifies both simultaneously.

Filter 2 FM control
The Cutoff frequency of Filter 2 can be modulated by the sine wave of oscillator 1.

Processing tips to reduce CPU usage
- Filter 1 uses less processing power than Filter 2. If you only need one filter, use Filter 1.
- Filter FM uses more CPU power.
- Drive uses more CPU power, especially when the filters are in series.

Info

For more on filter types see the Chapter 5.

Tip

The ES2 is very powerful. It uses up more CPU power than other Virtual Synthesisers.

Section 4 – the Output stage and effects

The Volume control sets the overall output of the ES2. The Distortion setting has two types, Soft and Hard and a level control.

Figure 8.22
Volume control.

- Soft is a 'valve' or 'tube' like distortion, suitable for more pleasing distortion effects.
- Hard is a more Transistor like distortion for harsher effects.

The Tone control cuts or boosts the upper frequency (treble) part of the distortion.
    The stereo effects section can be used in the following modes. All three are modulation type effects.

- Chorus – a rich ensemble effect.
- Flanger – a sweeping effect.
- Phaser – another sweeping effect.

You can vary the intensity and speed of the effects using the two controls.

Section 5 – LFO (low frequency oscillator) section

The destination of the LFO, i.e. which part of the ES2 is modulated by the LFOs, is set by the Router. Commonly in synthesisers, you can use the LFO to modulate the Pitch of the Oscillators (vibrato), the Filter Cutoff (wah) and the Amplifier (Tremolo). The Router gives the ES2 much more flexibility, allowing many destinations for the LFO's modulation output.
    This is discussed in more detail below. The ES2 has two LFOs.

LFO 1
The LFO 1 is polyphonic – i.e. each note you play has its own LFO. The LFO is not phase locked. So when playing more than one note, each note's modulation may be slightly out of phase, adding to the richness of the modulation.

- EG – allows you to fade the LFO modulation in when values are positive. When they are negative, the LFO modulation is faded out. Use this for delayed vibrato.
- Rate – sets the rate of the modulation.
- Wave – selects the LFO waveform. They are from top to bottom.

    * Triangular
    * Sawtooth and Inverted sawtooth
    * Rectangular and Inverted rectangular
    * Two types of random wave

LFO 2
There is a rate control which can be set 'free; with positive values, or synchronised to the song tempo at negative values.
    LFO2 has the same waveforms at LFO1

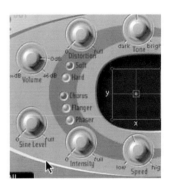

Figure 8.23
The LFO (low frequency oscillator) section.

Section 6 – Envelope generators (EG or ADSR) section

There are three envelope generators in the ES2. While ENV 3 is 'hard wired' to the output stage, i.e. it always controls the amplitude of a sound, the other ADSRs can be flexibly used in the Router. ENV3 can however be used as a modulation source in the Router.

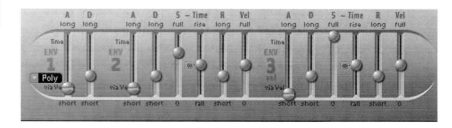

ENV1

This has three modes of retriggering – i.e. of starting the EG attack phase.

- Poly – every voice has its own Envelope Generator. When eack new key is played, the EG will retrigger.
- Mono – like the Legato setting. The EG is only retriggered when a previous note is released before a new note is pressed.
- Retrig – the EG is retriggered for every note held down whenever a new key is pressed.

The EG has two sliders (left):

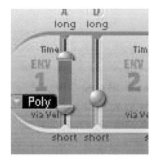

- Attack – the slider is split into two knobs. Setting these apart makes the Attack control sensitive to velocity. The top knob sets the attack time at maximum velocity, the lower the attack time at minimum velocity.
- Decay or Release. You can change this parameter to either a Decay or Release function by clicking on the D or R above the slider.

ENV2 and ENV3

These have identical controls:

- Attack – this has the dual knobs of ENV1, allowing it to become velocity sensitive.
- Decay – this is a standard decay control.
- Sustain and Sustain time – when the Sustain time slider is set to the centre, the Sustain slider acts like a normal sustain control i.e. the Sustain portion of the ADSR remains until the key is released.

  * If the Sustain time slider is set to a positive value it then sets the time the Sustain portion of the ADSR rises to maximum volume.
  * If the Sustain time slider is set to a negative value, the Sustain time slider sets the time it takes for the Sustain to reach zero volume.

- Release – this is a standard release control – it sets the time the sound takes to decay to silence after a key is released.
- Vel – this makes the whole ADSR sensitive to velocity. The Higher the value, the more sensitive to the velocity of struck notes. At zero, the ASDR is not sensitive to incoming velocity.

Section 7 – the Router

In many respects, this is the heart of the ES2. In conventional synthesisers, the LFOs, Modulation wheels and so on are 'hard wired' to the sections that they modulate – their sources.

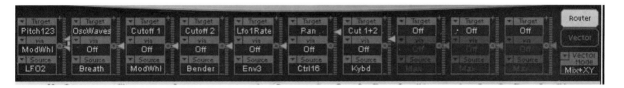

In the ES2, modulation sources and destinations are set in the Router. To see the Router, make sure that the Router button is selected (right).

Each Router has the following parameters:

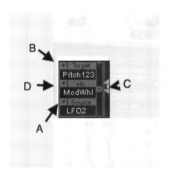

- Source (A) – this selects the modulation source. This could be, for example an LFO. Clicking and holding on the little triangle brings up a pull down menu (below left) where you can select the source.
- Target (B) – this selects the modulation destination. For example, you could choose Pitch 123 so the LFO modulates all three oscillators pitch (below right).

Info

You *must* set modulation destinations in the Router. Nothing is hardwired in the ES2.

Info

You can have up to 10 Router setups.

• Intensity (C) – the slider to the right of the Router unit sets the intensity of the modulation. Hold down the shift key while dragging the intensity control to move in finer steps.

Using the Via parameter

Via (D) – You can select a control for the Modulation source. For example, you could choose ModWhl so that the intensity is set by the hardware modulation wheel.

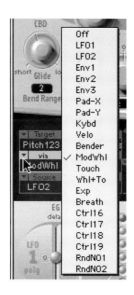

As you can see from the above there are many modulation Sources, Targets and Vias. When the Via is set to any value except OFF, the Intensity slider splits into two. The upper value sets the maximum intensity of the Via source (say, the Mod wheel), the lower value sets the minimum intensity.

There's more on the use of the Router later in this chapter.

Section 8 – the Square, Triangle and Vector mode

As we saw before the Triangle can be used to mix the levels of the three oscillators. The Square is similar, except that it can be used to control any modulation source.

To see the Vector mode, you need to make it visible by selecting the Vector button (above).

To get the feel of the Square, let's set it up like a virtual joystick to control the pitch of all three oscillators and the Triangle to control the relative volumes of each oscillator.

Manual Square control – using it like an on-screen joystick

- Select OFF as the Vector mode.
- Select the X target as PITCH123.
- Select the Y target as PITCH123 (right).

- Set the Int values to a non zero value (below left).
- Drag the joystick around to hear the effect (right). If you hold down the ALT key and click on the square the, control is centred.

You can do exactly the same thing with the Triangle. However, this always controls the Oscillator mix.

You can if you want use Logic's automation mode to record your mousings. However, you can also get the ES2 to control the Square and Triangle automatically using the Vector envelope.

Info

Setting the Square vector Router destinations to things like the pitch of oscillators, Filter cutoff and waves, you can then use the it to simulate the joystick effects so beloved of electronic musicians. Instant Dr Who!

The Vector envelope consists of 15 positions of the Triangle or Squares position that can be stored and then replayed over time – it's a recording of the cursor movements.

There are two types of positions – or points.

- Sustain points – if no loop is engaged, the envelope will stop at a sustain point until the key is released.
- Loop point – any point can be a loop. The looped area is the time between the loop and sustain points. You can have other points in between. The loops point means you can have a continuously moving sound.

Here's the default Vector mode display. Make sure SOLO POINT is not selected.

Creating a Vector point

Click on a point on the line while holding down the SHIFT key. You can see a new point has been added between point 1 and 2.

Deleting a vector point

Click on a point on the line while holding down the CTRL and ALT keys.

Giving a point a value on the Square or Triangle

Select a point and position the cursor as required.

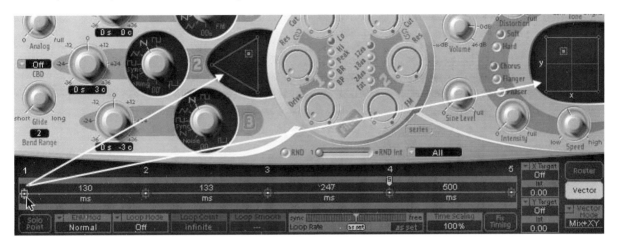

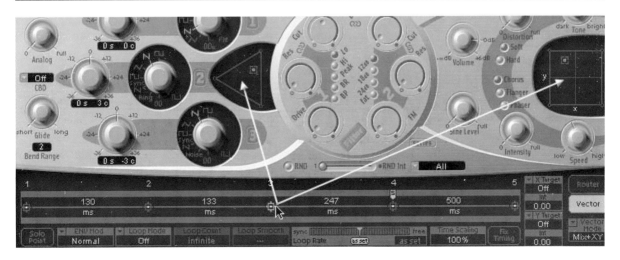

Re-setting a vector point to the default (centre)

Hold down the Alt key and click on the Triangle or the Square.

Setting the vector envelope times

Clicking on the time value and dragging the mouse up and down changes the time it takes for the envelope to travel to the next point. If you hold down the CTRL and Apple keys while changing the time, the following point time will shorten or lengthen to maintain their absolute positions.

Setting the Sustain point

Click on the bar above the point.

Setting the loop point

To set a Loop point, the Loop Mode must be set to something other than OFF. Click on the bar below the point, to set the point as a Loop point.

Other vector envelope parameters

Env Mode

- Normal – this affects the sound in various ways depending on the Loop setting.

  * If Loop is OFF, the Sustain point will be played as long as you hold a key. When you release the key, the Release phase of ENV3 will sound.
  * If Loop is ON and the Loop point is before the Sustain point, the loop will play as long as you hold a key.
  * If Loop is ON and the Loop point is after the Sustain point, the loop will be played after a key is released.

- Finish – this also depends on the Loop mode.

  * If Loop is OFF The Sustain point is ignored and the vector envelope will play even if you release a key.
  * If Loop is ON the loop will play regardless of the position of the sustain point.
  * If the Loop is ON and the Loop Count parameter is set to a value other than Infinite, the Loop will repeat that many times, then play the points after the loop.

Looping

The vector envelope Loops will cycle round the envelope you have set up, depending on the Loop parameters.

Loop mode

This can be set to Forward, backward or can go Forward to the Sustain point, then Backward – Alternate. If the parameter is set to OFF, the Loop plays once through.

Loop count

If this is set to Infinite, the Loop plays constantly (but see ENV Mod above). Or it can be set to play a fixed number of Loops.

Loop smooth

This smoothes out the transitions at the end of each loop as they cycle around. It's like cross fading in an sampler.

Loop rate

This sets the speed of the Looping. If you click on 'as set' the Loop plays at the speed set in the vector 'bar'. If you drag the slider to the right, you can change the loop speed. Moving the slider to the left, allows you to synchronise the loop with the song.

Time Scaling

This allows you to stretch or compress the whole vector envelope.

Fix timing

This rescales the loop to 100% – or as it was originally set.

Section 9 – the Random sound generator

This section allows you to generate new patches without programming. Some patches you make may be useless, some stepping points for tweaking and some genuinely useful sounds!

Info

The Loop mode must be set to anything but OFF for the Loop to be enabled.

It has the following parameters:

RND

Pressing this button changes the ES2 parameters in a random fashion. If you keep pressing, more randomization occurs. What is actually randomly changed depends on the RND destination setting.

RND intensity

This sets the amount of randomization. If the slider is set to the left change is minimized. If you drag the slider to the right, change is maximized.

RND Destination

You may only want to randomize some of the parameters of the ES2, say just the Filter or the LFOs, you can limit what is randomized using the pull down menu.

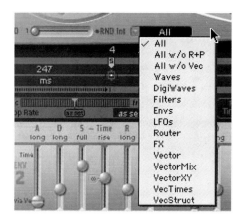

Some of these are self explanatory, however some are not.

- All w/o R + P – all ES2 parameters except all of the Router and the overall Pitch of the synth.
- All w/o Vec – all ES2 parameters except the Vector envelope.
- Waves – only the Wave and Digiwaves settings of the Oscillators are altered.
- Digiwaves – only the Digiwave types are altered.
- Vector – all vector envelope parameters are altered.
- Vector mix – only the Triangle cursor position are altered.
- Vector XY – only the Square cursor position is altered.
- Vector Times – only the time parameters of the Vector envelope are altered.
- Vector Struct – all vector envelope parameters are altered, even the loop and sustain points.

Using the ES2

Now we have covered the basic operating parameters of the ES2, we can turn to creating our own sounds. As the ES2 is a complex beast, it's useful to use the program to create some conventional synthesiser sounds, before moving on to the weird and wonderful.

Basic single oscillator per voice polyphonic analogue synthesiser

This sets out to emulate popular synthesisers like the Roland Juno series. The characteristics of these are the rather thin sound of the single oscillator per voice and the tone of the filter. This is usually beefed up by the on-board chorus.

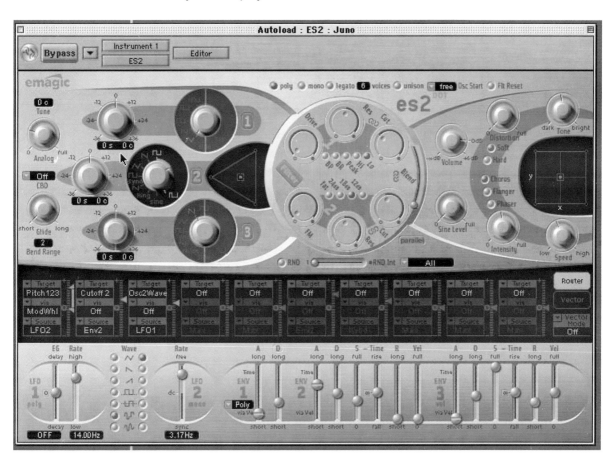

Main points of the sound

Oscillator 2 used only. Use the Sawtooth or Pulse width variable Square wave (picture below left). Filter 2 only is used (the blend control is set to that filter). Use a 12 or 18dB slope (pictured right).

Effect is set to Chorus and the Intensity is up with a medium speed.

The pitch of the oscillators are routed to produce vibrato using the Modulation wheel and LFO2. The rate is set with LFO2. Note the range of the Mod wheel (left). ENV3 controls the envelope of the volume as always. ENV2 is routed through to the filter Cutoff. Note the slow attack on ENV2 to create a filter sweep (below).

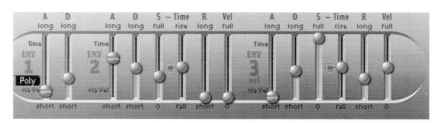

LFO 1 is set to produce Pulse Width Modulation of Oscillator 2 if it is set to use the variable pulse width wave. You change this intensity using the slider to the right of the Router unit (below left).

Number of voices set to 6 (right).

Options

Add a pseudo 'sub' tone an octave below using oscillator 1. Mix using the Triangle.

Add noise using oscillator 3. Mix using the triangle.

Use the Filter Resonance and Cutoff to taste.

Tip

Click and drag on the chain symbol to control both Resonance and Cutoff simultaneously.

Dual or Triple oscillator per voice polyphonic analogue synthesiser

This is a simulation of synthesisers such as The Sequential Circuits prophet 5, Roland Jupiter 8, Moog MemoryMoog and Oberheim OB8.

The characteristics of these synthesisers are a powerful fat sound. Usually a chorus effect is not needed.

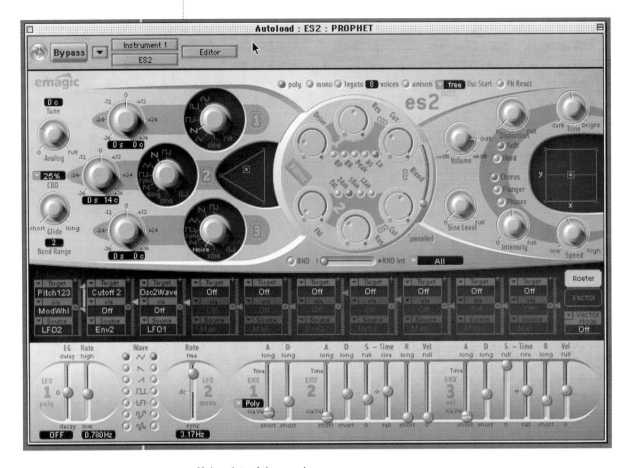

Main points of the sound

Two (or three if needed) oscillators are used. Use 1 and 2 for the sound and 3 for the noise. Mix with the Triangle. Detune Oscillator 2 to 'fatten up the sound' and use the CBD to reduce detuning artifacts as you play up the keyboard. Use triangle, sawtooth and square waves.

Filter 2 is used alone. Choose 24dB for the 'fat American sound' or 18dB for the 'Japanese tone'.

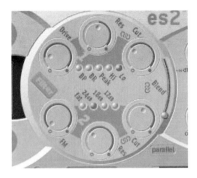

ENV3 is controlling the volume Envelope. ENV2 is set to control the Filter in the router. The Router is also set up to produce vibrato with the mod wheel and PWM of oscillator 2 when it's set to variable square waves.

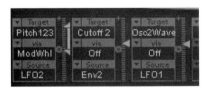

Number of voices is set to up to 8.

Options
If you set oscillator 2 to sync, bender range to zero and set the Pitch bend wheel to change the pitch of oscillator 2 only, you'll get the 'screaming lead' sound.

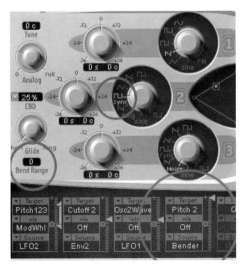

If you control the pitch of oscillator 2 using an EG the synchronisation will follow the settings. In the following figure, when you play a note the pitch of oscillator 2 will slide up and down according to settings of EG 1. However as oscillator 2 is synced to oscillator 1, what you will hear is oscillator 1 stepping through a series of harmonic changes. The EG 1 slider is split to make this effect velocity sensitive.

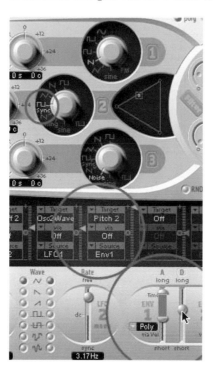

Info

When oscillator 2 is using the sync waveforms, its frequency is synchronised to that of oscillator 1. What this means in practice is that is you try to vary the pitch of oscillator 2, you produce a 'ripping' sound as it attempts to keep synchronised to oscillator 1.

You can use the Analogue knob (left) to add small variations to the sound making it appear warmer.

Basic digital synthesiser with or without filters

This (Figure 8.24) sets out to simulate the sounds of early digital synthesisers such as the Roland D50, Ensoniq SQ series, Sequential VS.

Main points of the sound

Use the setup above as a starting point. Use the Digiwaves of the three oscillators to produce non-analogue sounds. Or a mix of analogue and non analogue waves to fatten and warm the sound.

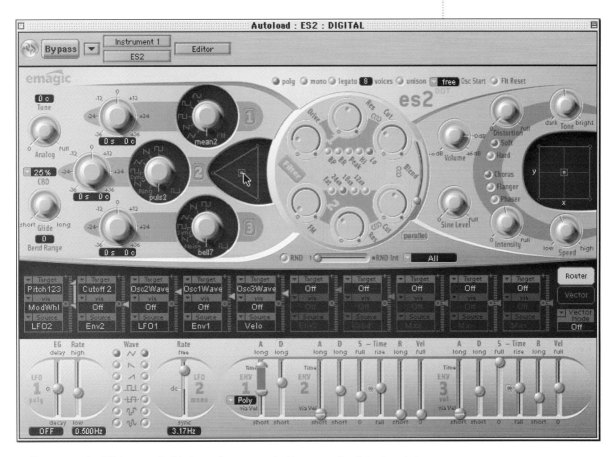

To access the Digiwaves, hold down the mouse button over the 'sine' and drag the mouse up and down. There are 100 Digiwaves (below left).

Early digital synthesisers didn't always have filters, so you may want to switch them out (middle pic), or use a thin sounding 12 or 18dB filter 2 (right).

Figure 8.24
Basic digital synthesiser with or without filters.

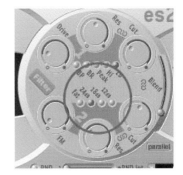

The Router has several blocks set up

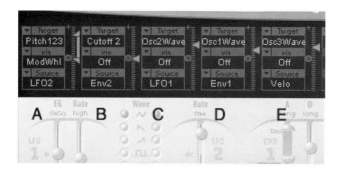

A This uses LFO 2 (Source) to modulate the pitch of all the oscillators (Target) using the Modulation Wheel (Via)
B This uses ENV 2 (Source) to change the level of the Cutoff (Target).
C This uses LFO 1 (Source) To change the DigiWaves of oscillator 2 (Target).
D This uses ENV 1 (Source) to change the DigiWaves of oscillator 1 (Target)
E This uses the Velocity of the keyboard (Source) to change the DigiWaves of oscillator 3

Use the Vector mode to fade in and out of the oscillators over time. Digital synthesisers often have individual Envelope generators for each oscillator.
    Here's how you do it.

• Select Vector mode. Make sure the Vector mode is set to Mix. Make sure Loop Mode is set to Forward and the Loop count to infinite. Make sure there are three points on the vector bar – delete points by clicking on one while holding the CTRL and ALT keys down. Add points by SHIFT clicking on the vector bar. Make sure the Solo point button is off.
• Set the loop start to the first position by clicking the bar under the point.
• Set the Sustain point at the last point by clicking on the bar above the last point.

• Click on point 1 to select it. Then drag the cursor on the Triangle to oscillator 1 (pic above right).
• Click on point 2 to select it. Then drag the cursor on the Triangle to oscillator 2 (middle pic right).
• Click on point 3 to select it. Then drag the cursor on the Triangle to oscillator 2 (pic below right).
• Change the times you want the sound to hold at each point. In this case 1000ms.

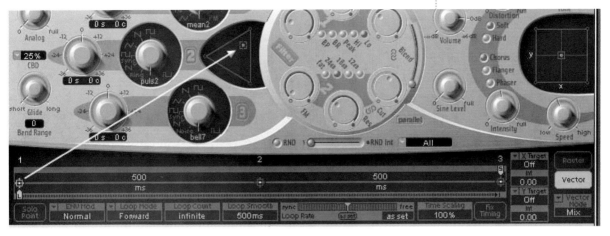

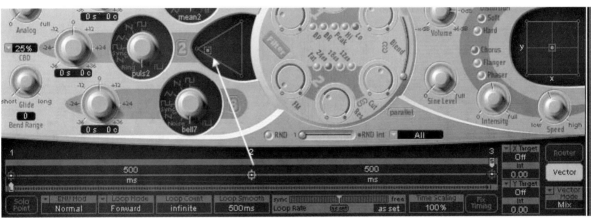

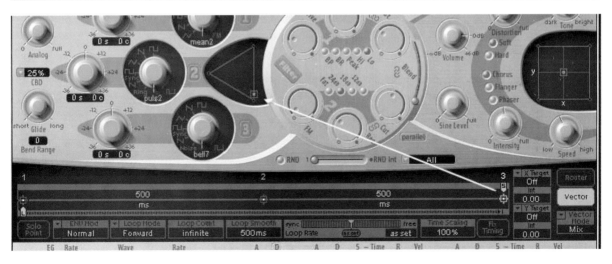

• Click on the time and drag the mouse up and down.

When you play a key, oscillator 1 will play for 1000ms and then fade into oscillator 2. Oscillator 2 will then play for 10000ms and then fade to oscillator 3, which also plays for 10000ms. The loop repeats until you release a key.

Options
Add a Chorus, Flanger or phaser to fatten and soften the sound.

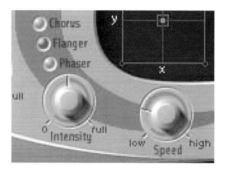

Add Logic audio reverb, echo or other effects. Digital synthesisers often have built in effects.

Digital wavesequencing synthesiser

In this type of synthesiser, digital waveforms are played in a sequence, stepping from one waveform to the next. An example would be the Korg Wavestation.

Main points of the sound

Oscillator 1 is set to the Digiwaves, the filter is switched off.

Switch on vector mode. Make sure the vector mode is set to XY. Create up to 15 vector points by SHIFT clicking on the vector bar. Set the Sustain point to the last point by clicking on the bar under it. Set the Loop point by clicking on the bar above the first point.

Make sure Loop Mode is set to Forward and the Loop count to infinite. Make sure the Solo point button is off. Set the time which you want each wave to play by clicking on the time value and dragging the mouse up or down.

Select Osc1Waves from the X and Y Target pull down menu. Set the Int of both to 1.00.

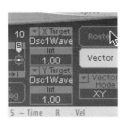

Click on Point 1. Move the Square cursor. Click on point 2. Move the Square cursor. Repeat for all the points.

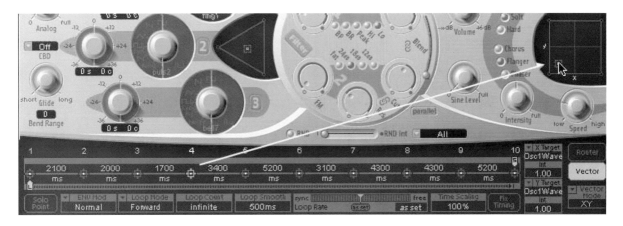

You can expand or compress the length of the overall loop using the Time Scaling value.

Now when you play a key, the ES2 will step through the Digiwaves of oscillator 1.

You can also modulate the Digiwaves using the Router. For example, using LFO 2 set to a random wave will cause oscillator 1 to randomly choose Digiwaves.

FM Synthesis

This technique produces tones similar to the Yamaha DX range of FM synthesisers. Start with the default patch, then modify as follows.

- When oscillator 1 is set to the area between the sine wave icon and FM, it can be modulated by the frequency of oscillator 2 – producing the distortion of a sine wave typical of FM synthesis.
- Set oscillator 1 to a position between the Sine wave icon and FM (left).
- Use the triangle to make sure only oscillator 1 is audible. Mute oscillator 2 and 3 (middle pic).
- Select a waveform on oscillator 2. Each one will produce a different sound. Now change the pitch of the silent oscillator 2. You'll hear the distinctive FM sound (right).

Tip

Use the Router or the Square vector envelope to modulate the frequency of oscillator 2.

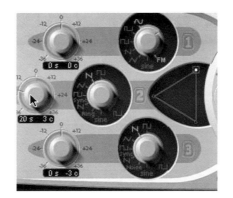

Miscellaneous ES2 features

Ring modulation

Ring modulation is useful for creating inharmonic bell like tones and clangs. The Ring modulator of oscillator 2 is fed by the output of oscillator 1 and a square wave from oscillator 2. The resultant output is a combination of the sum and difference frequencies of the input signals.

Here's how to use it. Use the Triangle so you can only hear oscillator 2 and set it to Ring (modulation).

Changing the waves of oscillator 1 will produce ring modulated tones.

> **Tip**
>
> Use the Router to modulate the waves and/or frequency of oscillator 1 while oscillator 2 is set to ring. You may also want to send oscillator 2 through ENV2 to produce bell-like envelopes.

Filter 2 FM

If Filter 2 is set to self oscillate, turning up the Filter FM knob creates ihharmonic sounds, useful for bell-like tones in a similar way to the FM synthesis of oscillator 1 (left).

You can modulate the Filter FM knob in the Router (right).

You can, of course, easily combine all of the above techniques to produce complex and original synthesiser tones. The ES2 rewards experimentation. And remember, you can use several ES2s in a song if your CPU power is up to it!

The EVOC 20

T he EVOC 20 is essentially a three part plug-in for the price of one! It is a vocoder and polyphonic synthesiser which is accessed from the Instrument plug-in slot on an Instrument object.

Figure 9.1
The EVOC 20.

The EVOC 20 TO is a monophonic pitch tracking vocoder which is accessed through the plug-in slot on any Audio or Instrument object. It's basically a plug-in like a reverb or compressor.

Figure 9.2
The EVOC 20 TO

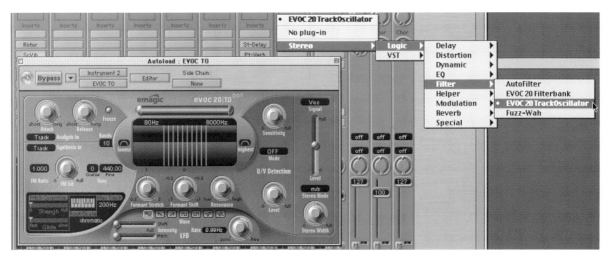

Figure 9.3
The EVOC 20 FB

The EVOC 20 FB is a formant filter bank which is accessed through the plug-in slot on any Audio or Instrument object. It's basically a plug-in like a reverb or compressor.

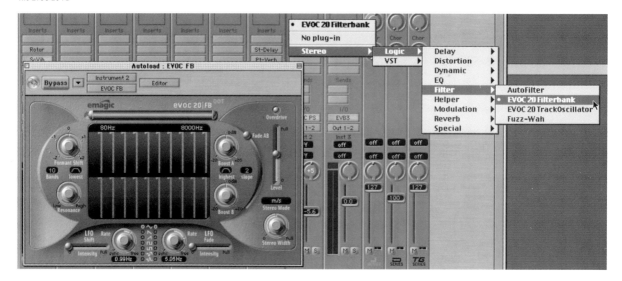

We'll look at each part of the EVOC in turn.

The EVOC 20 PS Vocoder/Synthesiser

Most people will have bought the EVOC 20 PS for use as a Vocoder. A Vocoder (VOiceEnCODER) allows you to impose the characteristics of an incoming audio signal (the 'analysis' input), which could be something like voice, onto a synthesiser sound (the 'synthesis' input). You can use any type of audio, including a live microphone feed, for real-time vocoding. Though the input signal has traditionally been a voice, you can use any kind of audio – drums, whole tracks – anything. The built in synthesiser of the EVOC can also be used as a stand alone polyphonic synthesiser.

You'll want to get Vocoding right away. Here's a quick start guide. You'll need a microphone to produce 'analysis' input. Connect it to your Audio interface. Lets say to input number 1. (If you don't have a microphone, see the section on using an audio file as the analysis input described below.)

- Open the Environment page. Create a new layer. Call it 'EVOC Live input' (Figure 9.4).
- From the New menu select Audio object.
- Double click on the icon. A normal Audio object will appear (Figure 9.5).
- Rename it 'Microphone live input' (Figure 9.6).
- Make sure the object is selected. Click on the Cha parameter in the parameter box and select Input 1 from the pull down menu (Figure 9.7).

Figure 9.4 (left)
Create a new layer.

Figure 9.5 (right)
A normal Audio object appears.

Figure 9.6 (left)
Rename it 'Microphone live input'.

Figure 9.7 (right)
Select Input 1 from the pull down menu.

- Leave the output box of the object to No Output – you don't actually want to hear your own voice mixed in! (Figure 9.8).
- Insert the EVOC 20 PS into an Instrument object in Logic audio (Figure 9.9).

Figure 9.8 (above)
Leave the output box of the object to No Output.

Figure 9.9 (right)
Insert the EVOC 20 PS into an Instrument object.

- Open an Arrange page. Select the Instrument object that contains the EVOC PS. The plug-in window will open (Figure 9.10).
- Select a Side chain input preset. Any will do (Figure 9.11).
- Now, click on the side chain button on the EVOC20 plug-in window. A pull down menu opens.
- Select the Input you have the microphone plugged into, in this example, Input 1 (Figure 9.12).
- Now play the keyboard while speaking into the microphone. You'll hear the distinctive vocoding sound.

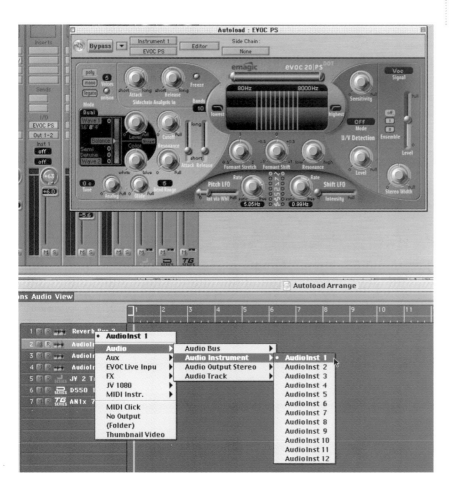

Figure 9.10
The plug-in window opens.

Select the EVOC 20 PS instrument.

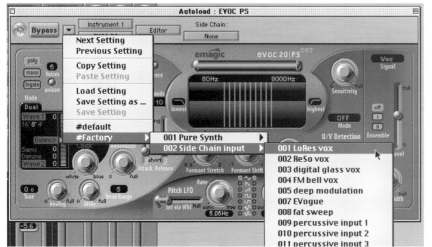

Figure 9.11
A pull-down menu opens.

Figure 9.12 (below)
Select the Side Chain Input you have the microphone plugged into

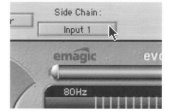

Recording the vocoded sound

Of course, you won't want to repeat this live performance every time you run through the track! What you need to do is record your microphone input as an audio file, then use this as the synthesis input as described in the section 'Using an Audio file as the analysis input'.

On the Arrange page select an Audio track. Audio 1 in this example. Make sure input 1 is in the Input box. If it's not, click on the Input box and choose input 1 from the pull down menu.

Figure 9.13
Click on the Input box and choose input 1 from the pull down menu.

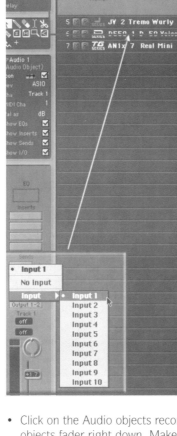

Figure 9.14
Make sure there is signal present.

- Click on the Audio objects record button – it should turn red. Pull the Audio 1 objects fader right down. Make sure there is signal present (Figure 9.14).
- Click on the audio 1 object track. Now click on the ECOC 20 PS instrument track while holding the SHIFT key down. Both tracks will be selected (Figure 9.15).
- Start Logic recording. Play the keyboard and use the microphone. The audio from the microphone will be recorded alongside the MIDI data for the EVOC 20 PS (Figure 9.16).

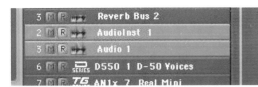

Figure 9.15
Both tracks will be selected.

Figure 9.16
The audio from the microphone will be recorded alongside the MIDI data.

- Click on the Audio 1 recording button to de-activate the recording input – otherwise you may get feedback!
- Drag the audio recording from audio 1 to audio 2.
- Select track 2 from the side chain pull down menu on the EVOC 20 PS (Figure 9.17.

Figure 9.17
Select track 2 from the side chain pull down menu.

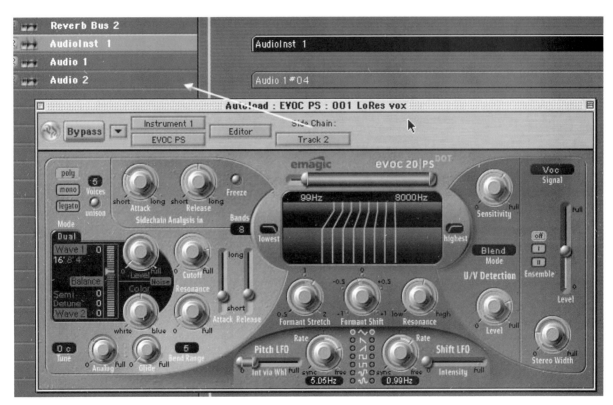

- Play back the audio. You'll find that the EVOC 20 PS will now be controlled by the recording.

Tip

If you get confused between Audio objects, such as audio 1,2 etc. and Track numbers, just select the View > Track Instrument channel arrange page menu item. You will now see the relevant track numbers on the Arrange page.

Figure 9.18

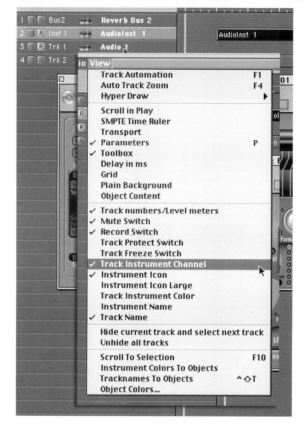

Info

Note that you have to speak and play. If you only do one of these, nothing will happen.

Tip

You don't just have to speak into the EVOC 20 PS! Try singing, clapping, finger popping and making all manner of strange noises. The EVOC synthesiser will take on the characteristics of the input sound. As you can imagine, this could produce some interesting effects if you run the whole of a track, a drum loop, a guitar or any other audio through the EVOC 20 PS.

If nothing happens when you speak and play, make sure you have an input into the Live Audio object – you should see the meter bar respond. If there is no input, check your connections. Also check that there is enough level coming into your Audio interface. Also make sure the EVOC 20 PS Instrument is selected in the Arrange page when you play the keyboard – it's easy to miss this one.

You may want to use headphones with the EVOC 20 PS when vocoding. Some settings can cause feedback through your monitors!

Using an Audio file as the analysis input

You can use any audio file or sequence in place of the live microphone input described earlier.

Place an audio file or sequence on a Track in the Arrange page. This could be a recording you have just done, or imported using the Audio>Import audio file main menu item. Ours is placed on Track 2 (Figure 9.19).

Figure 9.19

Insert the EVOC 20 PS into an Instrument object in Logic audio (Figure 9.20).

Figure 9.20

Open an Arrange page. Select the Instrument object that contains the EVOC PS. Open the plug-in window. (Figure 9.21).

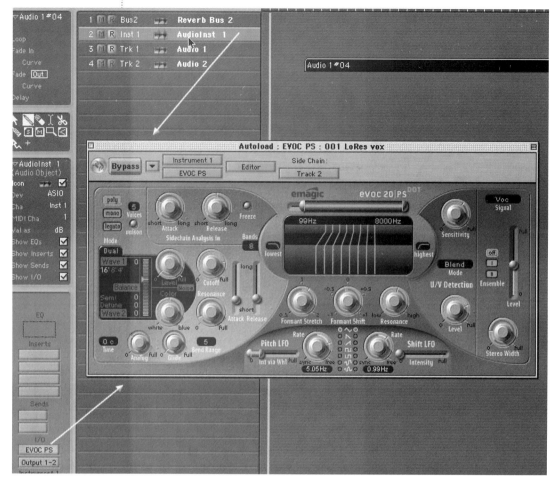

Figure 9.21

Select a Side chain input preset. Any will do.

Figure 9.22

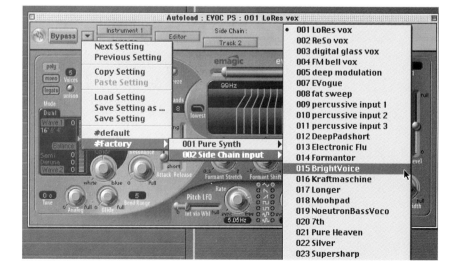

Now, click on the side chain button on the EVOC20 plug-in window. Select 'Track 2'

Now, start Logic Audio from the beginning of the sequence and play the EVOC 20 PS. You'll hear the distinctive vocoding sound.

Improving the quality of the vocoder effect
• Compress the side chain. Place a compressor on the audio file used as the Analysis input – compress as much as you can.

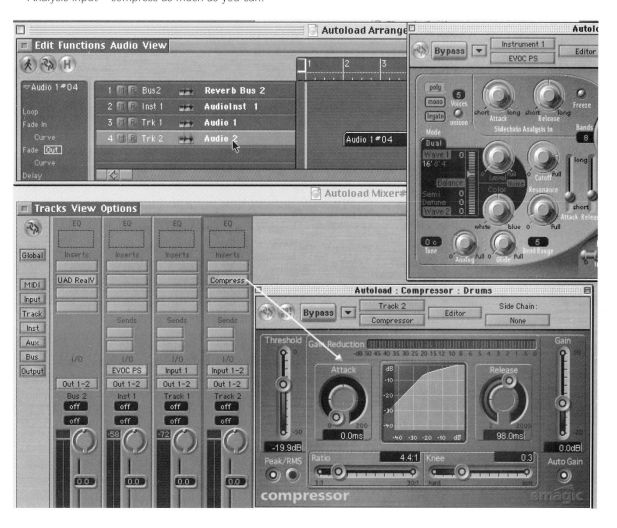

• Increase the high frequency output of the Analysis input using EQ.

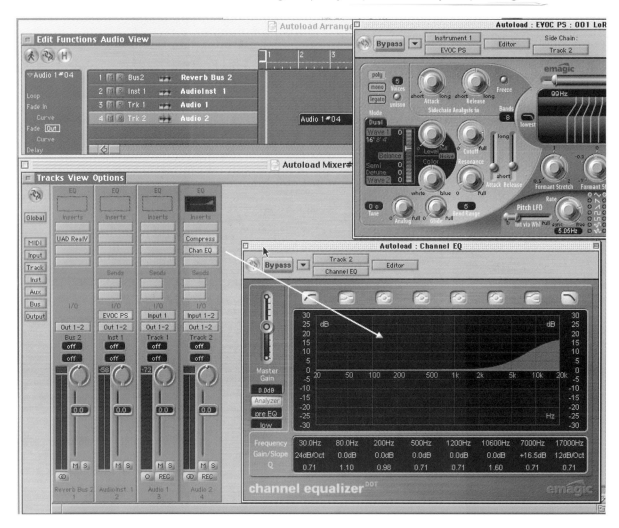

- Gate background noise of the Analysis input using a gate.

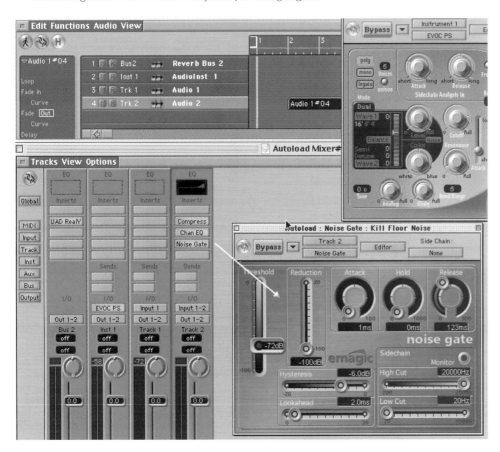

- Use a high sidechain Analysis Release setting to smooth out the sound.

The EVOC 20 PS in more detail

The EVOC 20 PS has two banks of band pass filters – the Analysis and Synthesis sections. Band pass filters only allow a small part of the frequency spectrum to pass through and cut out all frequencies above and below that band. The Analysis filter deals with incoming audio. The Synthesis filter deals with the synthesiser input.

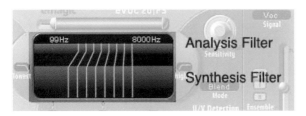

The EVOC band pass filters can have up to 20 bands. Both Analysis and Synthesis sections always have the same number of bands and these are connected together.

The signal path through the EVOC

The audio signal is passed to the Analysis input, and is divided into up to 20 bands. Each filter band has an associated Envelope follower. For each band, this Envelope follower tracks the amplitude changes within the band, producing control signals proportional to the volume.

These control signals are then sent to the corresponding linked Synthesis filter bank. They then control the levels of these banks, making the Synthesiser filter output an 'analog' of the Analysis signal.

Voiced and unvoiced sounds (U/V)

When we speak, vowels and consonants are produced in different ways. Vowels tend to be tonal sounds, while consonants contain a higher noise level. Vowels are said to be 'Voiced' while consonants are said to be 'Unvoiced'. To improve the intelligibility of the vocoded signal, the EVOC can differentiate between these sound inputs .If this U/V detector detects Voiced inputs, it passes the signal directly to the Synthesis filters. If the EVOC detects unvoiced components it can deal with this signal depending on the setting of the U/V detection Mode parameter (left).

- Off – unvoiced sounds are sent directly to the Synthesis filter input.
- Noise – unvoiced sounds are replaced by a noise signal.
- Noise + Synth – unvoiced sounds are replaced by a noise signal mixed with the Synthesis. Filter input.
- Blend – the unvoiced component of the sound is passed through a high pass filter to cut out the higher lower frequencies. This filtered signal is then mixed with the EVOC 20 PS output.

Use the level knob to adjust the amount of this replaced signal.

The Sensitivity knob sets the response of the U/V detection. Turning the knob to the right increases the recognition of the unvoiced portion of the input signal. However, too much of the unvoiced signal can swamp the voiced portion, leading to more noise.

Programming the EVOC 20 PS in side chain mode (Vocoder)

Section 1 – The filter bank

This is the heart of the EVOC 20. The upper half shows the Analysis filter section, the lower the Synthesis. All the changes you make to the parameters in the Filter section will be reflected in this graphic.

Bands

This selects the number of filter bands.

High/Low frequency

Sets the highest and lowest frequencies allowed to pass into the filter section. Any frequencies above or below this band will be cut. To change the values, click and hold on the silver knobs at the ends of the bar. You can drag the bar, moving both knobs together. Or you can change the numbers directly.

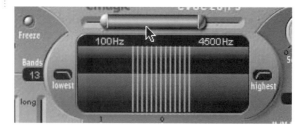

Info

Try changing the number of bands in the Filter bank. You'll see that the more the number of banks, the clearer the input audio sounds in the output of the EVOC 20.

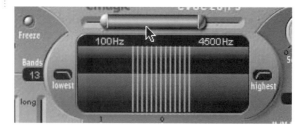

Lowest and highest

You can change the lowest and highest bands from the default band pass type to a High pass filter at the upper end or a Low pass filter at the lower end.

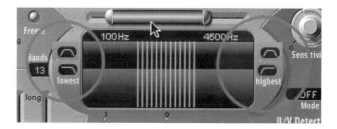

Formant stretch

This alters the relationship of the Filter banks in the Synthesis section with the Analysis section.

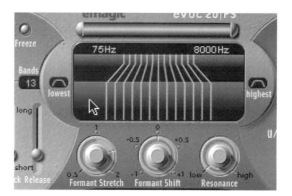

At a value at 1 the Synthesis bands are the same as those in the Analysis bands. Varying the value stretches or compresses the Synthesis banks in relationship to the Analysis bands. At low values the synthesis engine outputs a 'thin' sound.

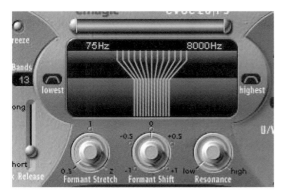

Formant shift

This control moves all the Synthesis bands up and down. At higher settings the Synthesis engine outputs a higher pitch sound.

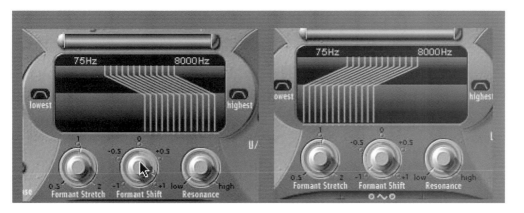

You can use these controls to vary the harmonic content of the Synthesis signal with respect to the input. For example, inputting a low voice and turning the Formant shift towards +1 makes the Synthesis output produce higher frequencies.

Resonance

Increasing the value of this control emphasises the middle frequency of each band. Low settings make the sound softer, higher value make the sound harsher.

Section 2 – polyphony

- Poly – in this mode, you can play several voices simultaneously. The maximum number of voices is set by the 'Voices' parameter.
- Mono – only one voice at a time can be played. The Envelope generator and Glide are retriggered even if the previously played key is still held down.
- Legato – only one voice at a time can be played. The Envelope generator Glide are retriggered only when a previously played key is released.
- Unison – the effect of this depends on the setting of the above buttons.
- Poly – each note played on the EVOC 20 uses two voices. The doubled voices are detuned by the amount set by the Analog Parameter.

Mono or legato

Up to 16 voices, the number set in the Voices parameter, are stacked onto one note.

Section 3 – the Oscillator, Filter and Envelope section

The EVOC 20 has two oscillators and there are two oscillator modes.

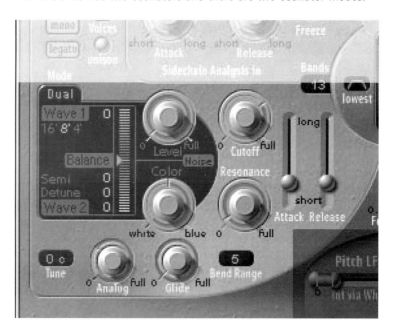

- Dual – the two oscillators produce digital waveforms to provide the Synthesis sound source. This is similar to a 'normal' synthesiser.
- FM – this is a two operator FM (Frequency modulation) sound source. Oscillator 1 is the carrier, using a sine wave. Oscillator 2 in the modulator, using any of the digital waveforms.

Wave 1 parameters

You can set the oscillator to three different pitches, 16', 8' and 4'.

The number to the right of the Wave is the Digital wave number. You can select from 50 waves. Click and hold the mouse over the number and drag up and down to change the value.

Wave 2 parameters

This oscillator also has 50 digital waveforms, selected in the same way. The Balance slider sets the level between the oscillators.

The Noise Level knob adds noise to the signal. The Noise Color changes the harmonic content of the Noise. White noise has the same energy over the frequency range (often used for wind and rain). Blue noise has the low frequency content removed.

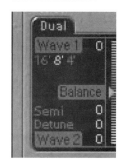

- Semi – this adjusts the tuning of the Wave 2 oscillator in semitone steps. Use the mouse to drag the values up and down.
- Detune – this adjusts the tuning of Wave 2 in percentage steps. 100% = one semitone.

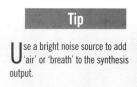

FM synthesis

The principles of FM synthesis are covered in more detail in Chapter 5. It produces a more digital tone, often with a bell like quality. It works on the principal of modulating a sine wave (the carrier) with another waveform (the modulator).

To change to FM mode, click on the Mode button.

Note that the oscillator parameters change.

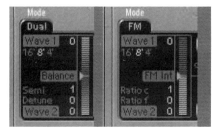

- Ratio C(oarse) – adjusts the coarse frequency ratio of Wave 2 to Wave 1.
- Ratio F(ine) – adjusts the fine frequency ratio of Wave 2 to Wave 1.
- FM int – determines the intensity of the sine wave modulation of Wave 1 by Wave 2. You can select any of the Wave 2 waveforms to do this. Higher FM int values produce more complex waveforms.
- Cutoff and resonance (left) – standard Low pass filter controls for roughly shaping the tone of the sound.
- Attack and Release controls (middle pic). The Envelope Generator. These affect the amplitude of the oscillators as a key is pressed.
- Miscellaneous oscillator parameters (right).

- Tune – this sets the overall pitch of the EVOC 20.
- Analog – alters the pitch of each note randomly and attempts to simulate the instability of analogue synthesisers. When it's on Full, the EVOC 20 can sound out of tune.
- Glide – sets the time it takes for one note to sweep up pitch to another. Its effect depends on the poly/mono/legato settings as described earlier.
- Bend range – sets the range of the MIDI controllers Pitch Bend wheel range in semitones.

Section 4 – Side chain analysis

These parameters control the Analysis input i.e. the live microphone input or audio file input.

- Attack – determines how fast each Envelope follower dedicated to each Analysis filter band reacts to incoming signals that are rising in volume. Longer Attack times mean that the EVOC 20 PS has a slower response to sudden increases in volume.
- Release – section D – determines how fast each Envelope follower dedicated to each Analysis filter band reacts to incoming signals that are falling in volume. Longer Release times mean that the EVOC 20 PS has a slower response to sudden decreases in volume.

- Freeze – captures the current Analysis spectrum. It's a kind of snapshot of the spectrum. When Freeze is set, any further input is ignored, as are the Attack and release parameters.
- Bands – sets the number of frequency bands. The greater the number, the clearer the input signal sounds when you play the EVOC 20.

Section 5 – The LFOs

The Pitch LFO controls the pitch of the oscillators to produce vibrato. Its intensity is controlled by the modulation wheel.

Int via Whl – this sets the upper and lower levels of LFO intensity when you use the Modulation wheel. The Right hand knob sets the maximum effect of the Wheel. The left hand knob sets the minimum effect of the Wheel.

The Rate knob controls the speed of the LFO modulation. Turned to the right, the modulation runs free. Turned to the left, the modulation is synced to the song tempo. You can select from the seven waves (right) to produce different vibrato effects.

LFO 2 is hard-wired to modulate the Formant Shift parameter of the Synthesis filter to produce phasing-like effects. The wave and rate knobs work in the same way as LFO 1. The Shift LFO intensity slider sets the amount of modulation of the Formant Shift.

Section 6 – Unvoiced/Voiced detection (U/V)

This section was discussed earlier in the chapter.

Section 7 – the Output section

- Signal – this parameter has a pull down menu where you can choose the following. It defines the signal you will hear from the output of the EVOC 20 PS.
- Voc – you will hear just the Vocoder effect.
- Syn – you will hear just the Synthesis output.
- Ana – you'll hear just the Analysis input. Normally this parameter will be set to Voc. The Syn setting makes the EVOC 20 PS into a polyphonic synthesiser.
- Ensemble – these three buttons produce a chorusing effect. Ensemble 2 is a richer version of Ensemble 1.
- Level – sets the overall output level of the EVOC 20.
- Stereo width – distributes the output of the Synthesis filter in the stereo field. When the control is set to 0 the output is monophonic i.e. all bands are centred. When the control is set to centre position, the lower frequency bands are output from the left channel, the higher frequency bands from the right. When the control is set to full, the bands are output alternately in the left and right channels, creating a complex stereo output.

Using the EVOC 20 PS as a polysynth

If you set the signal parameter to Syn, the EVOC 20 PS will behave as a normal synthesiser. You can use either the Digital waves from the oscillators, or the FM mode and the Filter and AR. For more on synthesisers, see the chapters on the ESM, ESE and ESP, ES1 and ES2.

The EVOC 20 TO pitch tracking oscillator

This is a vocoder equipped with a monophonic pitch tracking oscillator. This allows the EVOC 20 TO to follow a monophonic input, say a voice or flute. This input will be mirrored by the Synthesis output.

   The EVOC 20 TO is a plug-in, like a reverb or compressor. It's inserted into an Audio object in an insert slot.

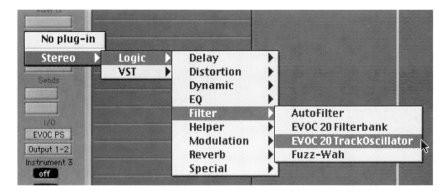

   Try inserting the EVOC 20 TO and playing back a monophonic audio file. Select different presets from the 'Pitch Tracking' menu and see what kind of effect they produce. Most of the presets say weather they should be used on percussive or vocal audio files. Please feel free to ignore this and try any of the EVOC 20 TO presets on any audio file!

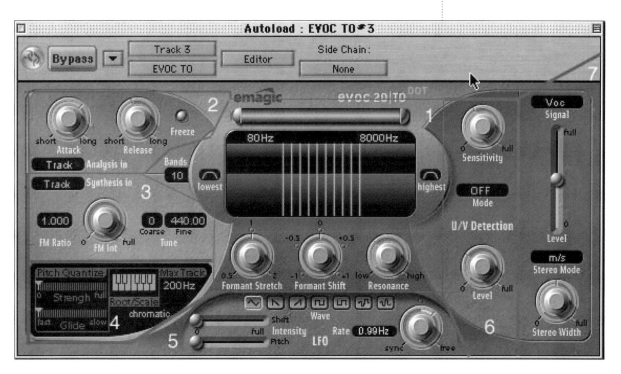

The EVOC 20 TO can also produce vocoder effects without a keyboard controller. As you can see, the EVOC 20 TO is similar to the EVOC PS Vocoder. Please refer to the section on the EVOC PS where stated.

Section 1 – The Filterbank
This is exactly the same as the EVOC PS.

Section 2 – Side chain analysis
This is the same as the EVOC PS with the following exceptions:

- Analysis In – this has a pull down menu.

- Track – you can use an audio track as the analysis source signal. This is the 'tracking oscillator' mode.
- Side chain – you can use an audio track on the side chain in exactly the same way as the EVOC PS. This is the 'vocoder' mode of the EVOC PS. More on this later.

Section 3 – The oscillator

This generates the basic sound of the EVOC 20 TO. It's a two oscillator FM system where one oscillator is the carrier, the other the modulator.

- FM int – if this knob is full to the left, the Tone generator outputs a sawtooth wave. Turning it to the right turns it into a FM Tone generator. The coarse and fine tuning parameters control the pitch of the Tone generator.
- FM ratio – this parameter sets the ratio between the carrier and modulator. With even numbered values, harmonic sounds are generated. Odd numbered values produce inharmonic or metallic sounds. The FM ratio parameter is active only when the FM int control is NOT set to zero.
- Synthesis In – determines the Synthesis input source.

The pull-down menu has the following parameters.

- Track – uses the audio track of the Audio object into which the EVOC 20 TO is inserted as the Synthesis source.
- Side chain – allows you to use another audio track the Synthesis source via the side chain.
- Oscillator – the EVOC TO uses the inbuilt tracking Tone generator as the Synthesis source.

Section 4 – Pitch quantize

This section controls the automatic pitch correction of the EVOC 20 TO. This attempts to keep the EVOC 20 TO in tune with the input signal.

- Strength – sets the automatic pitch correction intensity. At zero, no pitch correction occurs. When full the maximum pitch correction is used.
- Glide – sets the speed at which the EVOC 20 TO takes to correct the pitch. If it's set to Fast, pitch correction is rapid. Set it for slow to produce slurring effects.

- Root/Scale – sets the musical scale that the EVOC 20 TO is set to. For example, if the source input is in the key of C minor, select C and m in the Root/Scale parameters. To change these values, use the mouse to hold and drag the values.
- If you select user, you can create your own scale by clicking on the little keyboard.

- Max track – cuts the high frequencies of the Analysis signal helping the pitch detection algorithm to be more accurate. Set it to the lowest possible setting to produce consistent results.

Section 5 – the LFO

The EVOC 20 TO has one LFO that can modulate the pitch of the Tone generator and the Formant shift parameter of the filter. The intensity of this modulation is set by the two sliders. You can select from the seven LFO waveforms. The rate knob runs free when turned to the right, or is synchronised to the song when turned to the left.

Section 6 – Unvoiced/Voiced detection (U/V)

This is identical to the section in the EVOC PS

Section 7 – the Output section

This is also identical to the EVOC PS except there are no Ensemble settings.

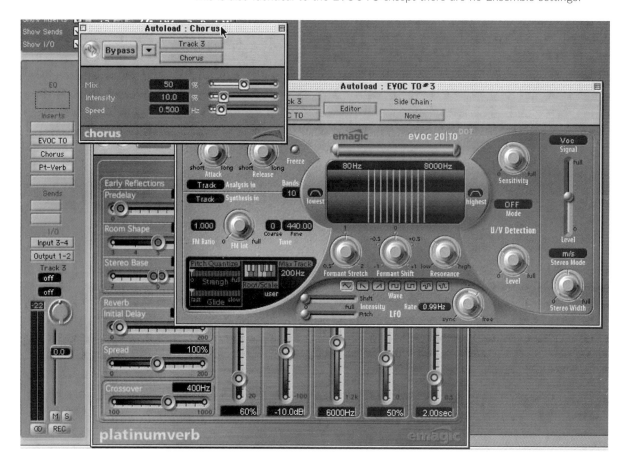

Info

Use Logic's modulation and reverb plug-ins alongside the EVOC 20 TO (above).

Using the EVOC TO in 'vocoder' mode

Insert the EVOC 20 TO plug-in onto an Audio track (Figure 9.21).

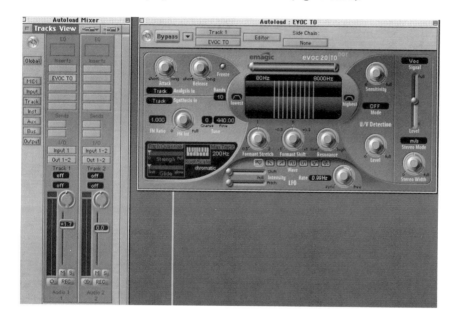

Import an audio file. Place it on an same track. Import another file and place it on the adjacent track. If you don't want to hear this track, turn its fader fully down.

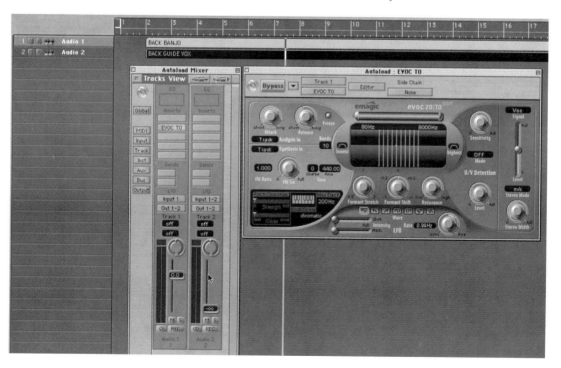

Info

Tracking oscillator effects are hard to predict. Don't be afraid to experiment or use the many presets.

Select 'Side chain' as the Synthesis in Source.

Select the modifying track in the side chain box

Now the audio file playing back on the EVOC 20 TO track will be modulated by the effects on the EVOC 20 TO of the second track. Try out some of the 'side chain' presets.

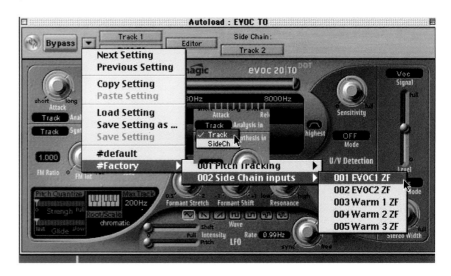

The EVOC 20 FB Filter bank

You can use the EVOC's powerful filter as a plug-in to process audio files or Instruments – even the EVOC PS!

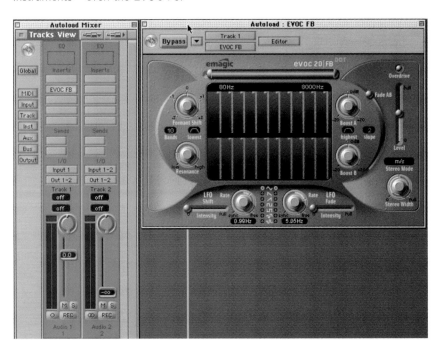

The presets show some of the effects that the EVOC 20 FB can produce.

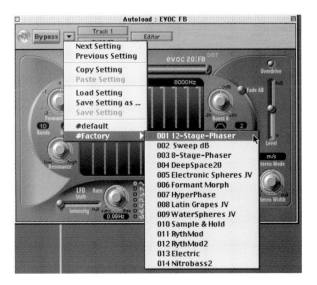

The EVOC 20 FB in more detail.

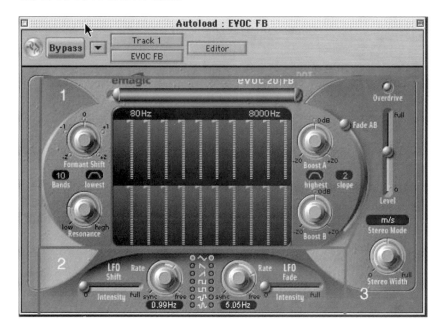

Section 1 – The Formant filter

There are two filter banks A and B. The number of bands is set using the band parameter. The level of each band can be set by dragging the small triangle at the top of each band, giving fine control over each band.

You can also draw filter curves by dragging the mouse across the filter graphic. The Bar at the top of the Filter block (right) sets the upper and lower limits of the Filter. Frequencies outside this range are muted.

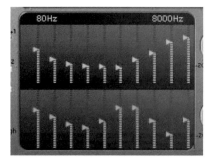

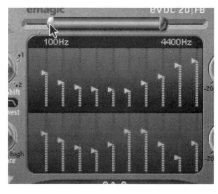

The low and high filter types allow you to change the filters at the extreme limits from bandpass to low and highpass.

- Slope sets the slope of all the filters.

  1 = 6dB/octave
  2 = 12 dB/octave

- Boost A/B allows you change the overall gain of the two filter banks. Use positive values to boost the signal if you are using the Filter to cut the level of frequencies, use negative values to Cut the signal if you are boosting frequencies.
- Fade AB control sets the balance between Filter A and Filter B.
- Formant shift moves the positions of all the frequencies up or down.
- Resonance – increasing the value of this control emphasises the middle frequency of each filter. Low settings make the sound softer, higher value make the sound harsher

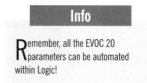

Section 2 – modulation

The EVOC 20 FB has two LFOs. The one on the left modulates the Formant shift. The one on the left modulates the Fade A/B fader. The intensity sliders sets the amount of the modulation.

Section 3 – the output

- Overdrive – creates a distortion effect. You may have to boost the levels of the Filter banks to hear the effect.
- Level – controls the overall output volume of the EVOC FB
- Stereo mode – has a pull down menu.

  * m/s – choose this mode if the sound being processed is monophonic.
  * s/s – choose this mode when processing stereo signals. In this mode, the two channels are processed by separate filter banks.

- Stereo width – this distributes the output of the Synthesis filter in the stereo field. When the control is set to 0 the output is monophonic i.e. all bands are centred. When the control is set to centre position, the lower frequency bands are output from the left channel, the higher frequency bands from the right. When the control is set to full, the bands are output evenly in the left and right channels,

Physical modelling

T he synthesisers within Logic are digital recreations of real analogue instruments. In computer terms they are 'modelled' on real life hardware. But computer modelling is capable of much more than recreations of old synthesisers. With a powerful enough computer and clever programming, other instruments can be modelled.

In a sampler, virtual or hardware, the sounds of original instruments are recorded digitally and then played back at different pitches via MIDI. While samples can have great realism, it's hard to get a sampled sound to play with real world nuances. Just pick up a guitar and play the same note several times. No two sound the same. This is one of the main reasons why real instruments have such interesting sounds. While sample players have become more sophisticated and attempt to simulate these nuances by having many samples spread across the keyboard and cross fading between several samples them to produce velocity sensitivity, they are always just playing back fixed recordings.

Physical modelling takes another route. The software mathematically describes not only the sounds, but the way the sound changes as it is played. So with 'non synthesiser' physically modelled instruments you won't find oscillators or filters – you'll find parameters describing the damping of tines on electric pianos, the position of pickups on a clavinet or the aging of the circuitry of an organ.

Physical modelling takes up a lot of CPU power. However, Emagic's instruments are written to minimize their demands while producing complex sounds.

The next chapter covers Emagic's physically modelled Instruments.

The EVP88 Piano

T his is a virtual modelling Virtual Instrument capable of recreating popular Electric Piano sounds and associated processing. Both the sounds and feel of the instruments have been modelled.

Programming the EVP88 is relatively simple. First insert it into an Instrument channel. Select the Piano model from the knob at A. Choose the number of voices to maximise CPU usage. (B). The more voices you choose, the more the CPU is used up. The model can then be processed using the remaining controls. The models all have different characteristics:

- The Fender Rhodes models all have the characteristic bell like tone. Lots of jazzers use the Rhodes, but a lot of modern instrumental and R&B music has also re-discovered the sound. The models are based on modifications that have been made to the original real-life instrument.

- The Wurlitzer models have a similar tone to the Rhodes. It's a harder sound, less bell-like and has a shorter sustain when a key is pressed.
- The Hohner Electra models are based on a relatively obscure German electric piano which is similar in tone to the Rhodes.

As trying to describe a sound is like smelling sunlight, I'd recommend you listen to each of the models in turn. Once you've chosen the basic sound, you can use the other controls to modify it.

C   The decay determines the time the sound falls to silence when you press a key. Full to the left is a fast decay, full to the right a long one. The more to the left the more percussive the sound.

D   The Release control determines how long the sound continues when you release a key. Full to the left is the slowest decay for a 'fast' sound. Full to the right is a long release.

E   Turning the Bell control more to the right increases the 'Bell-like-ness' of the tone. It adds odd harmonics to the higher frequencies.

F   The Damper control simulates the sound of the noise caused by the damper on the metal tines of the original pianos when a note is released.

G   The Stereo control spreads the keyboard notes across the Stereo field. Move this knob to the right to increase this effect. At the full setting, bass notes come from the left speaker, treble to the right, either for effect or for different processing using Logics Plug-Ins. Turn the control to the left for more 'accurate' piano sounds.

H   The Stretch controls attempt to simulate the stretches in tuning that acoustic piano tuners need to do to make the musical intervals appear in tune. When set to zero the tuning is equal tempered, i.e. each octave is the same frequency apart. Electric pianos are happy with equal tempered tuning as they don't have strings and thus these controls are more of an effect, or where the EVP88 seems out of tune with a recorded acoustic piano.

I   The warmth control adds slight deviations to the equal tempered tuning in an attempt to simulate the instabilities of a real instrument. Extreme settings of these controls can make the EVP88 sound out of tune! This could be a nice effect in certain circumstances.

J   These are simple tone controls adjusting the bass and treble levels of the sound – rather like the simple ones on an inexpensive stereo. These controls boost or cut the level of certain fixed frequencies which are determined by the Piano model used.

K   The Drive control attempts to simulate the tube amplifier that electric pianos are often played through. The Tone control selects the dominant frequency that is then distorted by the Drive control. The EQ controls (J) come after the Drive controls in the signal processing chain. So you can still brighten up a 'dark & distorted' tone.

L   The Phaser adds a classic guitar-style phasing effect to the EVP88. You can also use the Logic Audio Phaser Plug-In for more controlled and extreme effects. The Speed controls the rate of the Phasing. Setting it to 0 turns the Phaser off. The Color control increases the intensity of the phasing as you turn the control to the right. The Sterophase control increases the 'stereo effect' of the Phasing. Full to the right causes the sound to sweep between left and right channels. Full to the left has a high intensity monophonic phase that has equal intensity in both speakers.

Tips

For a classic Wurlitzer sound, choose a Wurlitzer model, set the Tremolo Rate to 55Hz, Sterophase to 0 and select a desired intensity.

For a classic fender Rhodes sound through a Fender twin amplifier, select a Rhodes model, set the Tremolo rate to 55 Hz and Sterophase to 180 degrees. Select a desired intensity. You may also want to try setting the Drive tone to 'dark' and dial in some Gain for the valve distortion effect.

Info

Don't forget you can add any of Logic's effects plug-ins to an Instrument channel.

Info

For more precise equalization use the EQ plug-ins within Logic.

M The Tremolo effect is similar to the Phaser except that it is the volume that is modulated.

* The Rate control determines the speed of the volume modulation.
* The Intensity controls determines how deep the volume changes are.
* If the Stereophase control is turned full left, the Tremolo is in mono. If it's full to the right the effect sweeps from left to right speaker.

N Turning the Chorus control to the right increases the intensity of the fixed frequency Chorus effect. This is often used on Rhodes sounds played on slow ballads. You can of course mix and match effects and EQ.

If you're interested In the history of the pianos modelled by the EVP88, there are many sites on the Internet dedicated to them. See Appendix 2 for more details.

The EVB3 Organ

Organs have been one of the mainstays of the music world for many years. The most popular model of the last few decades has been the Hammond tone wheel organ. This uses spinning electromagnetic wheels to produce sine waves, which are then mixed using drawbars to produce more harmonically complex tones. It's a kind of early additive synthesiser. The basic sound of the organ is further modified by vibrato and scanner chorus. You can also add a percussive harmonic to the sound. The real life Hammond organ also has an upper and lower keyboard along with a set of bass pedals, all of which can have different sounds.

The output of the Hammond is then usually sent to a rotary speaker cabinet – the most famous of which was made by the Leslie company. This usually has a rotating horn speaker for the treble end and a rotating baffle around a bass speaker for the lower. This produces a complex mixture of amplitude and Doppler shift vibrato. The rotary cabinet can usually run at a two speeds, fast and slow. The amplifier in the most desired Leslies were driven with valves, producing interesting distortion effects when their inputs were overdriven.

As the Hammond's got older, their key contacts got dirty, creating a click when a key is pressed, adding to the attack of the note. Players also often ran their organs through effects units, such as distortion, wah wah and chorus.

Other popular organ sounds were generated by transistor circuitry. While these were often seen as producing thinner tones, they have also become popular over the years.

The EVB3

The Emagic EVB3 is a physically modelled emulation of the Hammond B3 – the most sought after organ. The interface has a graphical recreation of the original organ. However, Emagic's programmers have added extra controls over the organ tone, allowing the model to recreate classic organ tones not only of the B3, but other types as well.

To hear the range of organ tones produced by the EVB3, check out the presets that come with the Instrument.

Info

You don't need two keyboards and a pedal board to play the EVB3! You can play the Upper drawbar settings over the range of your master keyboard, you can split the keyboard so you can play Upper, Lower and Pedal sounds across the range . You can even use two MIDI controller keyboards and a MIDI bass pedal unit to play each drawbar setting, emulating a real organ.

The EVB3 in more detail

Section 1 – tone generation

The graphical representation of the drawbars are the heart of the EVB3. You'll see that they are grouped into three sections – Upper, Lower and Pedal. These refer to the Upper and Lower keyboards of the organ, the Pedal to the pedal board. Drawbars are inverted faders each producing a sine wave of different pitches. The intensity of the sine wave increases as you pull out the drawbar.

The pitches are, from left to right on the Upper drawbars side. The fundamental is the root note of the organ. i.e. if you play a C note, the fundamental is a C too.

16'	Sub octave fundamental
$5\,^1/_3$'	Sub octave third harmonic
8'	Fundamental
4'	Second harmonic
2'	Third harmonic
$2\,^2/_3$'	Fourth harmonic
$1\,^3/_5$'	Fifth harmonic
$1\,^1/_3$'	Sixth harmonic
1'	Eighth harmonic

Info

The frequencies are given in feet ('). This is a leftover from church organs where the pitch of the pipes making the sound was given in feet.

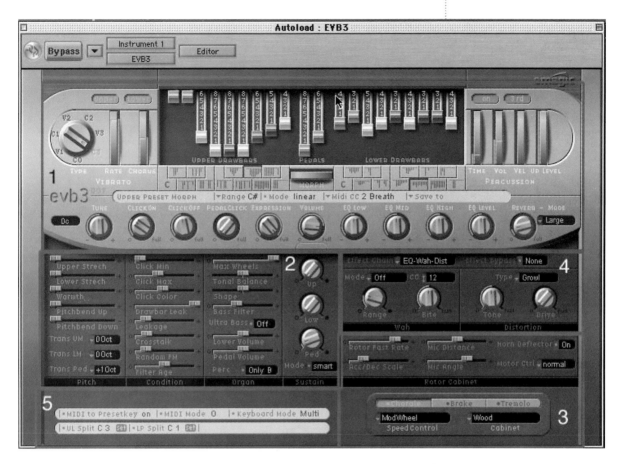

The Vibrato section has a rotary switch (below left) for choosing several types of Vibrato (V*) and Scanner chorus (C*). You can turn the effect on and off for individual keyboards. There are also two sliders setting the Rate of the vibrato effect, and the level of the chorus.

The Percussion section (right) controls the addition of a rapidly decaying harmonic 'click' when you first play a key. The percussion effect is polyphonic. However, if you play a new key while another is held down, the percussion is not played.

- On – turns the percussion effect on. The button to the right selects the percussion harmonic. Choices are second or third harmonic. The four sliders set the following parameters
- Time – sets the time of the decay of the percussion effect. Set to a low value for a more percussive sound.

- Vol – sets the level of the percussion sound.
- Vel – sets the velocity sensitivity of the percussion effect. At high values, the percussion will have less of an effect when a key is played softly.
- Up Level – sets the volume of the Upper drawbars allowing you to balance them against the percussion signal.

Presets

The original B3 had some drawbar setting presets which were selected by reverse colour keys at the lower end of each keyboard. The EVB3 has emulations of these.

As you can see, they are laid out in the style of a musical keyboard. Clicking on a preset will change the drawbar settings.

Upper preset morph – Drawbar morphing

You can use the Morph wheel under the drawbars or a MIDI controller to fade between two Upper drawbar presets.
- Range – sets the range of the morph. It also turns off the morphing. For example, setting the range to A will morph the presets at C, B flat and A.
- Mode – the morph can be preformed in a linear fashion, where the drawbars move smoothly from one setting to another, or Step, where they move in small intervals.
- MIDI cc – sets the MIDI controller to be used for controlling the morph via a hardware controller.
- Save – saves the current preset.

Various tone parameters
- Tune – sets the overall tuning of the EVB3 in cents. 1 semitone = 100 cents.
- Click on – sets the simulation of the key click when an key is pressed. The higher the value, the more the effect.
- Click off – sets the simulation of the key click when an key is released. The higher the value, the more the effect.
- Pedal click – sets the simulation of the key click when an pedal note is played.
- Expression – sets the maximum level of the expression controller if you are using an expression pedal.(MIDI controller number 11)
- Volume – sets the maximum level of the volume controller if you are using an volume pedal.(MIDI controller number 7). Also sets the overall volume of the EVB3.
- EQ – simple low, medium and high tone controls, similar to those on a Hi-Fi.
- EQ level – sets the level of the EQ settings on the sound. Turn the knob full left to have no effect, to the right for the full effect.
- Reverb – the pull down Mode menu selects between Reverb types. The original B3 had a spring reverb.

The knob sets the level of the Reverb.

Section 2 – Physical model parameters

This section allows you to vary the parameters that make the up the physical model of the EVB3.

Pitch
• Upper stretch – stretches the tuning of the upper keyboard as you play up the keyboard.
• Lower stretch – stretches the tuning of the Lower keyboard octave as you play up the keyboard.

These two parameters will make the keyboard sound out of tune when played octaves apart. However, it may help it to be in tune with an acoustic piano.

• Warmth – introduces random tuning deviations into the EVB3 to simulate the non linear nature of the real instrument.
• Pitch bend up and down – set the range of the pitch bend wheel on a MIDI controller keyboard. A real B3 has no pitch wheel, but if you play the keyboard while turning the organ off and on you get a variable pitch bend effect. Use these sliders and the pitch bend wheel to simulate this.
• Transpose – vary the octave and key settings of the three organ sections separately.

Condition
Organs change their tonal characteristics as they age. These parameters attempt to simulate these effects.

• Click min and max – set the upper and lower range of the click effect caused by dirty keyboard contacts.

- Click color – sets the tone of the click. Turn the slider more to the right to brighten the click.
- Drawbar leak – attempts to simulate the high frequency noise that is in an old B3's signal output. Turning the slider to the right increases this effect.
- Leakage – adds another high frequency inharmonic distortion to aid the realism of the model. Turning the slider to the right increases this effect.
- Crosstalk – simulates the intermodulation distortion of a real organ. Turning the slider to the right increases this effect.
- Random FM – creates random frequency modulations of the tine bars. As theses are sine waves, this results in slight harmonic shifts, simulating the aging of the tonewheels.
- Filter age – another tonal effect that occurs as the organ ages. Use the slider as a tone modifier.

Organ

- Max wheels – sets the maximum number of tone wheels used to simulate the organ sound. The more wheels used, the more accurate the sound. However, this also uses up more CPU power.
- Tonal balance – moving this slider to the left creates a brighter, less bassy sound. Moving it to the right creates a baser more muted tone.
- Shape – distorts the sine wave output of the tone wheels. This parameter is used to simulate other organ types. Turning it to the right brightens the sound, adding harmonics.
- Bass filter – moving this slider to the left reduces the bass frequencies of the Pedal drawbar sound. Moving it to the right enhances the bass sound and makes it grittier.
- Ultra bass – creates a deep bass boost on the pedal drawbars.
- Lower volume – sets the balance of the lower drawbars to the Upper.
- Pedal volume – sets the balance of the pedal drawbars to the Upper.
- Perc – when set to always, the UP Level in the Percussion section is available to balance the drawbars. When set to Only B, the Percussion section/Upper drawbar mix simulates a real Hammond B3.

Sustain

These three controls set how quickly the organ sound decays when you release a key. Organs usually have a very fast decay – no sustain. However, turning the knobs to the right increase this sustain level.

- Mode – this has two parameters. Smart makes sure the sustain doesn't get out of hand at high settings. This is the usual setting. Normal is useful for producing more in-harmonic tones.

Use a slight sustain if playing bass pedals to make the sound more fluid.

Section 3 – the Rotor cabinet

These parameters affect the 'Leslie' simulation of the EVB3. A rotary speaker is usually something like the diagram on the right.

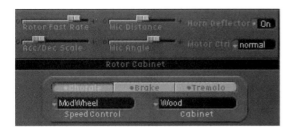

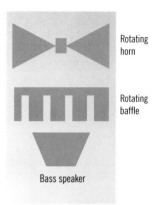

Rotating horn

Rotating baffle

Bass speaker

- Rotor fast rate – sets the speed of the fast rotary speaker effect.
- Acc/dec Scale – sets the rate at which the rotary speaker speed sup and slows down when you swap between the two speeds. If the slider is full left, the speed change is instantaneous. Move it to the right and the change is slower and more like a real rotary speaker.
- Mic distance and Mic angle – change the positions of the virtual microphone from the virtual speakers!
- Horn deflector – simulates the effect of removing the mechanical baffle of the horn rotor to produce more Tremolo effect and less Doppler.
- Moto ctrl – simulates the different type of motors of different Rotary speaker types. They all produce a slightly different modulation effect. For example the 910 mode simulates the effect of stopping the bass baffle, leaving the treble spinning.

Microphones

Rotor controls

You can select from the there rotary speaker speeds, Chorale (slow), Brake (stopped, but still passing through the amplifier circuitry) and Tremolo (fast).

The Speed control pull-down menu selects the way the hardware MIDI controllers affect the rotor speed.

Info

The rotor speed is usually changed by using the Modulation wheel on the controller keyboard. As the speed changes between fast and slow, you will hear the rotors slow down or speed up.

- Off – turns hardware control off
- Modwheel – when the wheel is fully down, the rotor speed is set to Chorale, when it's fully up it's set to Tremolo. In between it's set to Brake.
- Modwheel Toggle – pushing the wheel up once changes the speed to Tremolo. Pushing it up again changes it back to Chorale.

- Modwheel temp – similar to the first ModWheel setting but Brake is never set. It just swaps between Chorale and Temolo.
- Touch – pressing harder on a key on a controller keyboard that has touch sensitivity switches the rotor to Tremolo. Pressing down again changes it to Chorale.
- Touch temp – pressing harder on a key on a controller keyboard that has touch sensitivity switches the rotor to Tremolo. Releasing the pressure returns the rotor speed to Chorale.
- SusPdl Toggle – pressing down on the sustain pedal switches the rotor to Tremolo. Pressing it again switches it to Chorale..
- SusPdl temp – pressing down on the sustain pedal switches the rotor to Tremolo. Releasing the pedal returns the rotor speed to Chorale.

Cabinet

This sets several different emulations of rotary speaker cabinets. Different materials produce different tones.

Section 4 – the effects

- Effect chain – sets the order in which the effects are placed in the signal path. Changing this order can have a major influence on the sound of the EVB3. You can also Bypass the effects section with this pull down menu.
- Effect bypass – click on this box to allow separate bypass of the effects for the Pedal drawbars only.

Wah

- Mode – selects the wah model from the pull down menu.
- CC – sets the control of the wah to a MIDI controller number so you can use a pedal, for example, to control the wah effect.
- Range – sets the frequency range of the wah effect.
- Bite – enhances the high harmonics of the wah effect as the knob is turned to the right.

Distortion

- Type – selects the kind of distortion from the pull down menu.
- Tone – controls the tone of the distortion effect. Turning the knob to the right makes the distortion brighter.
- Drive – increases the level of the distortion effect.

Section 5 – miscellaneous functions

- MIDI to preset key – you can use the lowest controller keyboard keys to change drawbar presets on the EVB3. This switches this feature on and off
- MIDI Mode – the EVB3 drawbars can be controlled by the physical drawbars of organs such as the Hammond XB1 or the Roland or Korg models. These organs require slightly different controller types and the two MIDI modes set these. You'll need to consult your organ manual.

- Keyboard mode – set to Multi, the Upper drawbar voicing plays over the entire range of the controller keyboard. When it's set to Split, you can play all the three drawbar voicings on one keyboard.

Splitting the keyboard

You can split a keyboard into zones. These zones will then play the Upper, Lower and Pedal. Here's how to do it

Set the Keyboard Mode to Split. Click the SET button next to UL (Upper/Lower) split. It turns red.

Now play a key on your controller. The key name will appear in the display. This sets the split between the Upper drawbars (these will play to the right of the split) and the Lower ones (to the left of the split).

Click the SET button next to LP (Lower/Pedal) split. It turns red.
Now play a key on your controller to the lower end of the keyboard. The key name will appear in the display. This sets the split between the Lower drawbars (these will play to the right of the split) and the Pedal ones (to the left of the split).

You can now play all three drawbar settings from one keyboard.

Using more than one MIDI keyboard.

You can play each of the EVB3's drawbar settings from individual MIDI controllers. The Upper, Lower and Pedal drawbar sets respond to consecutive MIDI channels. Say for example you have two MIDI keyboards and a MIDI bass pedal controller.

- Set keyboard 1 to output on MIDI channel 1
- Set keyboard 2 to output on MIDI channel 2
- Set the MIDI bass pedal unit to output on MIDI channel3

Now you can play each drawbar set with its own keyboard – just like a regular organ.

Info

You'll need a MIDI merger or a UNITOR or AMT8 to 'mix' three separate MIDI controller inputs into Logic.

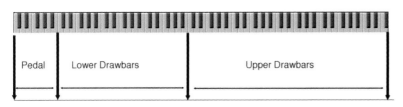

Using and programming the EVB3

To get an idea of what the EVB3 is capable of, we'll start with a basic organ sound with no effects.

Load the default preset (left). Some wit at Emagic has programmed in a virtual lid! Keep it closed for the moment.

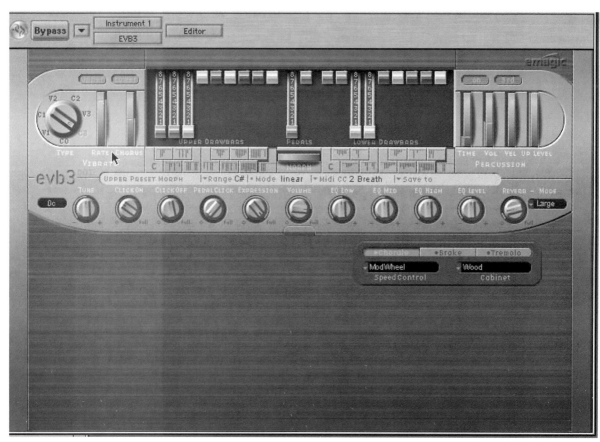

Turn off the Vibrato. Turn off the percussion. Set the rotary speaker to Brake. This stops the rotary cabinet.

Now, let's concentrate on the upper drawbars. Push them all the way in.

If you can still hear a whine, open the lid by clicking on the handle, and turn all the Condition sliders down.

Close the lid by clicking on the handle again. Bring out the third drawbar. This is the fundamental tone. Play a C note and listen to the pure sine wave. This is the basic tone for the EVB3.

Now bring in the lowest drawbar.

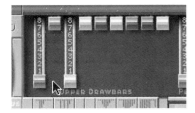

You can hear that this is set an octave below the fundamental. Now bring out the last drawbar. This is set an octave above the fundamental.

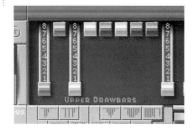

Push in all the Drawbars except the fundamental. Try drawing out the fourth, fifth, sixth, seventh and eighth drawbars each in turn, then pushing them back in. You'll hear that each produces a harmonic of the fundamental – it sounds like you are playing a scale.

Push them all back in again.. Now pull out the lowest drawbar and the third. Try pulling out the second drawbar. This again is a harmonic of the first.

These mixtures of sine wave are what makes the organ tone distinctive. Mixing the drawbars can produce some interesting tones. Try the following drawbar combinations and listen to the results.

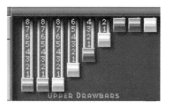 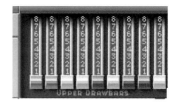

Info

The Lower drawbars are identical to the upper. The pedal section just has the fundamental and a single harmonic.

Making changes to the model

Open the 'lid' by clicking on the handle. Turn all the Condition sliders full to the left and the Organ ones to the centre.

Lets see what the aging characteristics do to the tone. Set the drawbars to the following:

Info

You may have to repress a key after changing a parameter to hear its effect.

- Try adjusting the Drawbar leak. This will add noise characteristic of an old Hammond.
- Try adjusting the filter age – this acts like a tone control.
- Try adjusting the Leakage and Crosstalk sliders. These also add noise depending on the pitch and harmonics in the tone.
- Turn the Click on knob fully up.
- Set the Click color slider to maximum to hear this effect better.
- Set the Click min to zero and the Click max to full (pic right).
- Play a key. You'll hear the clicking that is characteristic of old dirty organ key contacts. Try adjusting the Click color. A more muted sound, about a third the way up the slider is a good start point.
- Try turning up the Click off knob (right). This adds a click when you release a key.

While we have a 'pure' organ sound, try adjusting the Tonal balance and Max wheels parameters to see what effect they have on the tone.

Try adjusting the Shape slider. At the centre, the tone is more tone wheel based. Pulling the slider to the right allows you to emulate the cutting tone of a transistor organ.

Improving the sound

As you can hear, the sound produced by the drawbars alone is harmonically complex but pretty dull. We need some articulation! Switch on the Chorale setting of the rotary cabinet. You'll immediately hear a movement and richness to the sound. Make sure the Speed control is set to ModWheel. Use your controller keyboard's Modulation Wheel to change the speed of the rotary cabinet. You'll see the graphic buttons switch between Chorale, Brake and Tremolo.

- Try selecting different cabinet types (left). These acts as tone controls, modelling the different types of real-life cabinets.
- Try changing the speed of the Tremolo setting using the Rotor fast rate slider.
- Try changing the speed at which the rotor speeds up and slows down using the Acc/Dec scale.
- Try adjusting the mic placement sliders. Increasing the distance slider makes the sound more airy and open. The mic angle changes the tone of the sound.
- Try Changing the Motor Ctrl settings in the pull down menu (left). These change the way in which the cabinet spins.

Many organ sounds rely on vibrato. This, in combination with the rotary cabinet can create some very complex modulations.

Turn on the vibrato

Turn on the vibrato (left) and select one of the V settings (middle pic). Play a key – you'll hear the Vibrato effect.

Try changing the rate of the modulation (right pic).

Select a C setting. Increase the Chorus slider. The Chorus effect is a sound a little like Vibrato and Tremolo combined. This combined with a fast rotary cabinet Tremolo setting, is a classic organ tone.

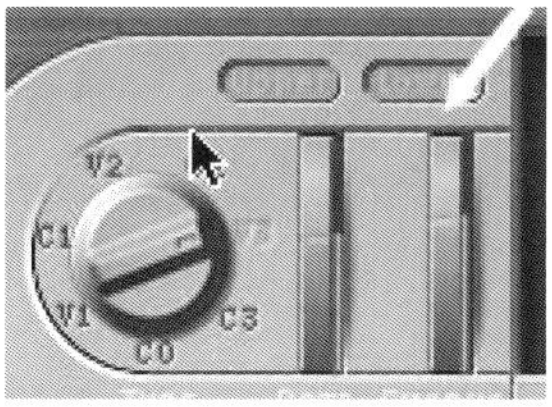

Now let's explore the percussion effect. This adds bite and articulation to the sound. First, switch off the Vibrato so you can hear the percussion effect more clearly. Then turn on the Percussion. Make sure it's set to 3rd by clicking on the button. Select the following drawbar settings shown in the left pic. You'll hear it more clearly with less high harmonics in the tone (middle pic).

Drag down the Up Level slider to mute the Upper drawbars (right pic). You'll just hear the percussion generator.

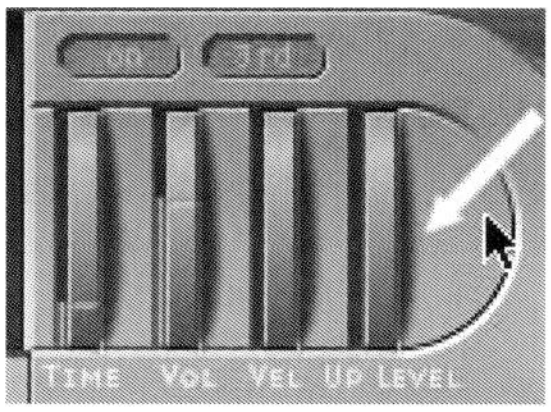

Turn the Vol of the percussion effect full up (left pic below). Turn up the Time slider (middle). This sets the length of the decay of the effect. Try a setting half way for now. Try the difference between the second and third harmonic percussion. Just click on the button (right pic).

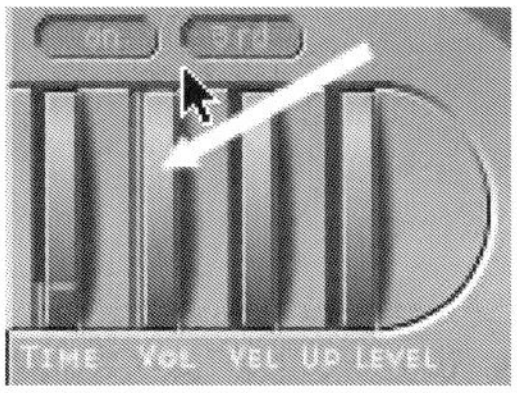

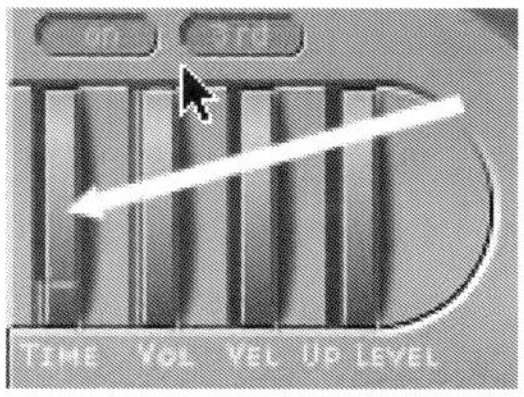

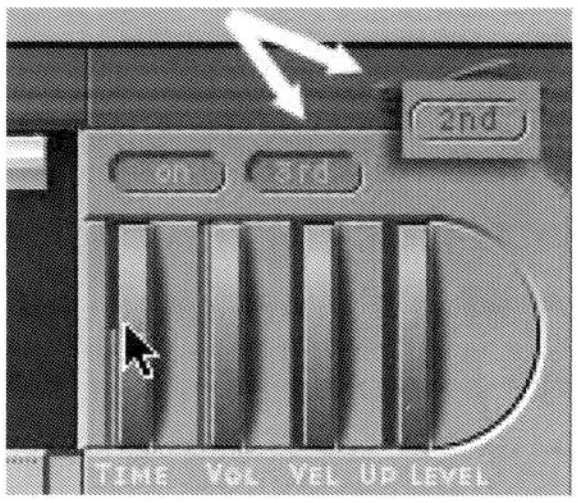

Turn up the Up Level slider to bring in the Upper drawbars. Mix to taste with the Vol setting.

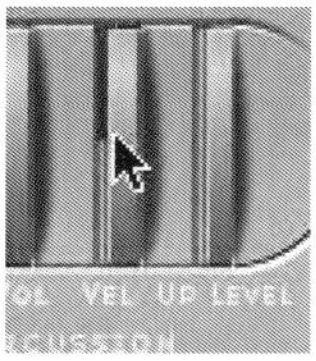

Info

A lot of the sounds we consider to be classic Hammond, are actually created by the rotary cabinet and its distortion.

Tip

Add lots of Click On and Off to enhance the percussion effect.

Info

The percussion effect is heard only when you release a key before playing any others.

Now let's dirty up this sound. Select Eq-Wah-Dist from the pull down menu. Set the distortion type to Growl.

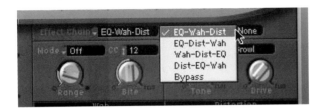 

Turn the Drive to full. Adjust the Tone to modify the distortion.

Now let's funk things up. Select the CryB setting in the Wah Mode pull down menu (left below). Set the CC to '1 Modulation wheel' by clicking and dragging the mouse up and down (middle pic). Select Touch from the Speed Control pull down menu (right). The rotary cabinet speed control is now set by aftertouch.

Set the wah range and bite controls as follows.

Tip

If you can set a Volume pedal on your MIDI controller keyboard to another MIDI controller number (not 7) you can then use this to produce the Wah effect by selecting it in the CC box.

The Modulation wheel on the keyboard controller now adjusts the Wah effect. Pressing down on a key produces the rotary speaker speed change (as long as your controller keyboard sends out aftertouch data.).

Emulating other organs

While the EVB3 has superb emulations of the Hammond tonewheel sound, It's perfectly capable of producing other organ sounds too. The main competitors of the Hammond all used transistor circuitry to generate their tones. These sounds are very different to the tonewheel sounds.

First listen to the presets supplied which demonstrates these tones. Load one of the Vox organs. These sounds are emulation of the Vox continental organs from the 60's.

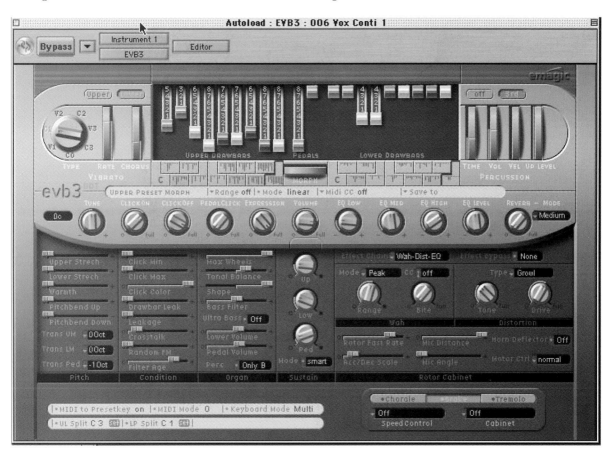

Main points of the sound

Rotary speaker is stopped (pic left below). These organs are rarely played through one. Set the Shape slider full to the right to distort the tonewheel tone (middle). The click color is set to the right, making a bright click as you press and release the key (right pic).

To hear this, the Click on and Off knobs are turned up. Use a drawbar setting with less low tones (left), and lots of brash bright harmonics. Some distortion colours the tone (mid). Organs of this period often have a bright, fast vibrato (right).

Using the EVB3 effects section as a plug-in
You can use the different EVB3 effects sections as a plug-in on Audio or other Instrument tracks. You can see the effects in the Modulation and Distortion section of the Logic plug-ins.

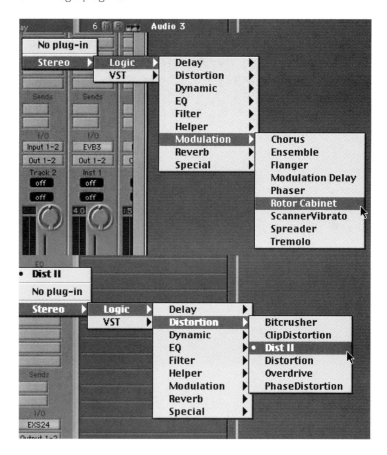

The effects are Rotor cabinet, Dist II and Scanner vibrator. Try inserting the plug-ins onto an Audio track or Instrument

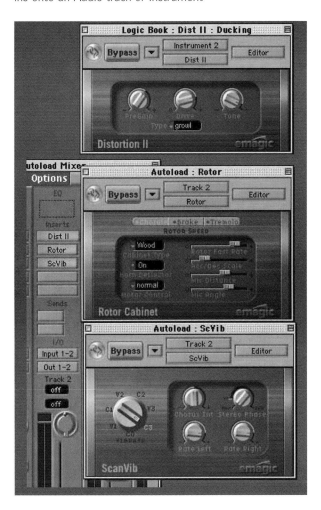

Try selecting the plug-in presets to see how they affect the sound.

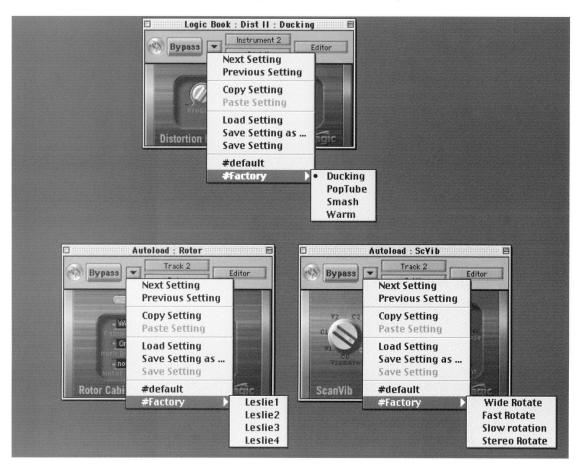

Tip

The Scanner vibrato and Rotary speaker plug-ins are really useful on other organ sounds. Try the fast speed on vocal tracks and the fast and slow on guitar tracks.

Rotor cabinet

The Rotor cabinet plug-in controls are identical to the section on the EVB3 described previously in the chapter.

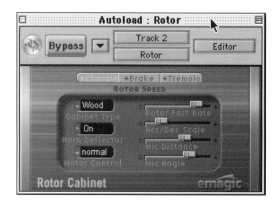

Scanner vibrato

The knob on the left selects the vibrato(v*) or scanner chorus(c*) types.

- Chorus int – sets the amount of the effect.
- Stereo phase – changes the phase of the chorus. The left and right channels are set out of phase, adding a tremolo-like portion to the sound.

There are separate Right and Left rate controls for setting the speed of the modulation effect.

Dist II

You can select between three types of distortion.

The Pre Gain knob sets the input level to the Drive. Selecting different combination will give you different distortion effects. Setting the Pre Gain high and the Drive low creates a warm, valve-like, sound. Turn the Pre Gain and Drive full up for maximum distortion.

The Tone control increases the treble portion of the sound.

The EVD6 clavinet

The EVD6 clavinet is a physically modelled virtual instrument based on the popular keyboards made by Hohner in the 1970s. The original instrument, the Clavinet D6, produces its sounds by a tight metal string being pushed onto an anvil when a key is struck. The end of the string 'short circuited' by the anvil is wound with yarn. This has the effect of damping the note when the key is released. This gives the D6 a Harp, guitar and Harpsichord like quality. The vibrations of the string are converted into an electrical signal up by electromagnetic pickups. This arrangement made the D6 very sensitive to the velocity and attack of the player's technique and therefore was a very expressive instrument.

While the D6 was made famous in the 1970s on countless funk records, it was often the extra keyboard of choice for players who already had the requisite Fender Rhodes, Hammond Organ and Mini Moog. For every Stevie Wonder who played a D6, there was a Gentle Giant.

The Clavinet D6 was often played through effects units to extend its tonal range. Common choices were wah wah, distortion and phasing. Because the sound of the D6 is quite guitar-like, using these effects allowed the keyboard player to produce some guitar-like pyrotechnics.

The Emagic EVD6

The EVD6 uses physical modelling to recreate this instrument. Unlike the original, which had few on-board sound modifiers, the EVD6 has control over many of the parameters that make up the sound. You can vary the pickup position, string damping, string decay and tension and many more parameters. There's also a in-built effects section that can be used as a plug-in on other Audio objects.

Insert the EVD6 into an Instrument object
As usual, the first thing to do is try out a few of the supplied presets to get a feel for the Instrument and the sounds it can produce (Figure 13.2).

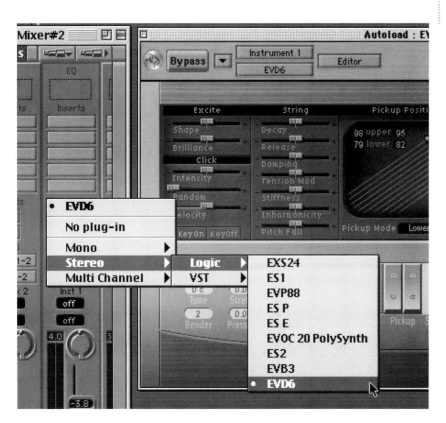

Figure 13.2
The EVD6 clavinet

Figure 13.2
Try out a few of the supplied presets

The EVD6 in more detail

Section 1 – pickups

These are the tone generating part of the D6. The graphic shows the pickup position across the strings. You can vary the pickup position by dragging the ends of the pickup bars, or dragging the upper and lower values directly. There's also a Pickup mode pull-down menu with the following options.

- Lower – only the lower pickup is used
- Upper only the upper pickup is used
- Lower – upper – the upper pickup sound is subtracted from the lower
- Lower + upper – both pickups are used, their outputs mixed.

Try playing the EVD6 and varying these pickup parameters. You'll find that a wide range of tones can be produced from just this section..

Section 2 – modifiers

These parameters adjust the physical model of the D6.

- Excite – this has two parameters. This adds a bright airy sheen to the EVD6 tone
- Shape – sets the frequency the Brillance controls boosts.
- Brilliance – sets the level of the exciter. Push the slider to the right to make the sound brighter.
- Click – sets the intensity of the click effect when a key is released. It Simulates the damper hitting the string.

- Intensity – sets the amount of click. Move the slider to the right for more click.
- Random – makes the effect act in an unpredictable fashion more like the real D6
- Velocity – makes the click effect velocity sensitive
- Key on – the click is heard when you press a key.
- Key off – the click is heard when you release a key.
- String – adjusts the characteristics of the EVD6 string models.
- Decay – adjusts the decay of the string. Moving it to the right increases the length of time the sound takes to fall to silence when you press a key. Dragging it to the left makes the length shorter. If the slider is full to the right, the sound plays for as long as you hold down the key in an 'organ-like' fashion.
- Release – sets the length of time it takes for the sound to decay to silence when you release a key. Moving the slider to the right increases the Release. If the Pitch fall slider up, the pitch will fall when you release a key.
- Damping – adjusts the damping of the string. The further to the right the slider, the more the muting.
- Tension modulation – simulates the pitch variation of a string has when it has first started vibrating – before it becomes stable. Moving the slider to the right, increases this effect.
- Stiffness – models the string stiffness. Moving the slider to the right increases the stiffness.
- Inharmonicity – allows you to add inharmonic characteristics to the sound. Moving the slider to the right increases this effect.
- Pitch fall – sets the pitch fall rate after the key has been released. You must set a long release time to hear this effect. Moving the slider to the right increases the effect.

Section 3 – keyboard
- Voices – sets the number of notes the D6 can play simultaneously. The more the voices used, the greater the CPU power used.
- Tune – sets the overall tuning of the EVD6 in cents
- Warmth – adds a random variation to the pitch of the D6 in an attempt to simulate a real mechanical instrument.
- Stretch – stretches the tuning of the EVD6, so that the octaves are slightly out of tune.
- Pressure – in the original D6, applying pressure to a key when it'd down will bend a string, producing a pitch variation. This parameter simulates this effect.

Section 4 – models, effects and output
- Filter – this is a basic, pre-set tone control that appeared on the original D6.
- Pickup – these switches have the same effect as the pickup mode in Section 1. You will see the values there change as you use the Switches. These switches were available on a real D6.
- Stereo spread – if you click and hold on this knob and drag the mouse up or down you'll see a representation of the stereo positioning of the sound at the output of the EVD6.

If you hold down the mouse over KEY and drag vertically, a blue band appears representing the spread of keys played across the stereo spread. If this is set at maximum, the low notes appear from the left speaker, the high notes from the right.

If you hold the mouse over PICKUP and drag vertically, a red marker appears representing the spread of the pickup outputs across the stereo field.

- Model – click and hold on the Model name. A pull down menu appears allowing you to choose from a series of Clavinet D6 models.

- Level – sets the overall output volume of the EVD6
- Damper (left below) – this is a graphic simulating the damper wheel on a real D6. Clicking and holding on this control and dragging the mouse up and down changes the string damping. It's a real-time version of the String damping slider in the String section.
- Damper Ctrl (right below) – you can control the Damper with a MIDI controller. The default is the Modulation wheel, but you can select another controller from the pull down list.

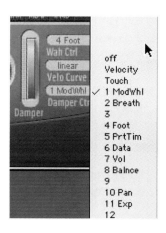

- Velo curve – sets the response of the EVD6 to incoming velocity from a keyboard. You can select from several different curves, or fixed levels.
- Wah ctrl – you can use the pull down menu that appears when you click on this parameter and use a hardware controller to adjust the wah effect. Most usefully, this would be a wha wah pedal-like foot controller for maximum funky reality!

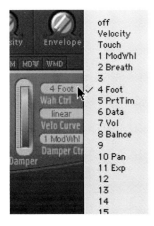

FX order

You can change the order in which the effects are placed. For example: WDM sets the EVD6 tones to play through the Wah section, the Distortion section and finally the Modulation section before being output.

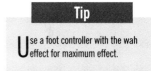

Distortion

- Comp – holding down the mouse and dragging over the parameter box allows you to turn off the effect or choose from several compression ratios. Use higher values for more compression, i.e. 20.0:1. Compression reduces level variations in the output of the EVC6 and increases average volume.
- Tone – adjusts the tone of the distortion effect. Turning the knob to the right makes it brighter.
- Gain – sets the level of the distortion effect. The higher the compression setting the greater the distortion.

Modulation

- Mode – holding down the mouse and dragging over the parameter box allows you to turn off the effect or choose from several modulation types.
- Rate – sets the speed of the modulation.
- Intensity – sets the amount of the modulation effect.
- Wah-mode – holding down the mouse and dragging over the parameter box allows you to turn off the effect or choose from several wah types. These are models of classic wah wah pedals.
- Range – sets the frequency range of the wha effect. Turning the control up lowers the frequency range.
- Envelope – sets the filter envelope of the wah effect. Set the control to half way for the maximum envelope effect.

Tip

Use a foot controller with the wah effect for maximum effect.

Info

All the EVD6 parameters can be automated, including the effects and pickup sounds.

Using the EVD6

Like many physical modelling Instruments, sounds are often best created by experimentation or modification of preset sounds. However, to get a feel for the EVD6 load in the 'default' preset and try the following singularly and in combination.

Select a different model and hear the sounds the basic tones produce.

Try varying the string parameters (left) and try moving the pickups (right).

Try adjusting the damper control. Set the Damper Ctrl to use the Modulation Wheel to adjust it. At high settings, the sound is like a guitar whose strings are muted with a hand (left). Try adding Distortion, wah and modulation. Try varying the arrangement of the effects (middle pic). Try adjusting the Filter and Pickup switches (right).

Using the EVD6 effects section as a plug in

The EVD6 adds a plug in to the list of Logic Audio plug-ins. It's contained in the Filter section. It's really useful for adding warm, fuzzy tones to audio files or virtual Instruments.

You can instance this in an Insert box on any Audio object. A plug-in window opens up – it's called Fuzz-wah.

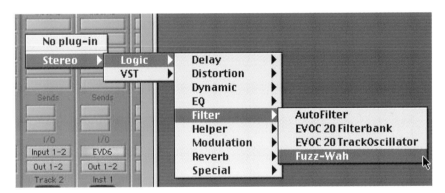

Import an audio file onto the track or Instance a Virtual Instrument and try out some of the presets.

Fuzz–wah controls

You can change the order of the effects. Wah into fuzz or fuzz into wah.

- Wah mode – selects the wah model.
- Auto gain – keeps the level of the wah effect constant.
- Relative Q – sets the centre frequency of the wah effect.
- Pedal range. Dragging the lower end sets the lower range of the wah effect when using a pedal. The upper end sets the upper range.
- Normalize – sets the pedal range to the same values as a 'standard' wah wah pedal.
- Autowah – you can get the plug-in to play a wah effect without using an external controller.
- Depth – sets the amount of the Autowah effect.

The Attack and Release controls set the envelope of the filter sweep. Set the controls to the left for a more pronounced wah effect.

Fuzz

- Comp ratio – sets the compression ratio . Turning up the knob increases the parameter, making the sound more compressed.
- Fuzz gain – turning up the knob increases the distortion effect. Set a high Comp ratio for maximum effect.
- Fuzz tone – turning up the knob increases brightens the tone of the fuzz effect.

Sampling

A sampler is just a computer that plays back digital recordings of real sounds. The first samplers were simple computers built into hardware, with specially written, dedicated, software. It was only a matter of time before samplers were incorporated into software on personal computers as 'soft' samplers.

Some sampling theory

Sampling is just a form of digital recording that is played back, usually, via MIDI. Like all digital recording, a sample is produced when an analogue signal is digitized via an analogue to digital interface. The signal is 'sampled' or broken down into a numerical description of that sound. Once in the digital domain it can be played back at different rates to give different pitches.

There are two important things to be taken into consideration when sampling a sound.

The sampling frequency

This determines the number of 'slices' taken of the analogue input source you want to record. Harry Nyquist, the mathematician, proposed a theorem regarding digital recording. The Nyquist theorem states that the sampling rate must be at least twice the value of the highest frequency you want to record. Failure to do this results in an audible artefact known as Aliasing. So, for example, if you want to digitise a sound with the highest frequency of 20kHz (around the upper limit of human hearing) you must sample at a frequency of at least 40kHz. This is why CD is sampled at 44.1kHz. Low rate sampling frequencies often have a distinctive 'grungy' sound, while higher rates are more true to the original recording.

Figure 14.1 (left)
Low sampling rate.

Figure 14.2
High sampling rate.

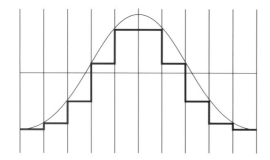
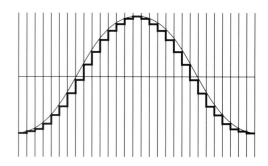

As you can see from the Figures 14.1 and 14.2, the higher the sampling rate, the more the waveform resembles the incoming analogue signal.

The bit depth

While the sampling frequency is concerned with the pitch of the sampled sound, the bit depth is concerned with the amplitude resolution. CD is 16 bit as it describes 65535 discrete values. A 4 bit recording system will have only 256. You can look at bit depth in the same way as resolution on a digital camera – the higher the bit depth the more 'in focus' the sound. In audio terms, the bit depth defines the dynamic range, measured in dB.

You can measure the dynamic range that will be given by a bit depth using the formula

6 x the number of bits

So a 16 bit system has a dynamic range of

6 x 16 = 96dB

Whereas a 4 bit system has a dynamic range of only

6 x 4 = 24dB

Figure 14.3 (left)
4 bit resolution.

Figure 14.4
8 bit resolution.

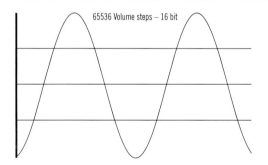
65536 Volume steps – 16 bit

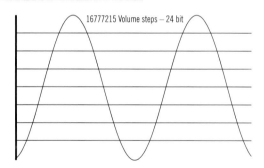
16777215 Volume steps – 24 bit

As you can see from the Figures 14.3 and 14.4, the greater the bit rate, the more discrete amplitude steps are described by the digitised waveform.

Once a sample is recorded and stored on disk, it can be reloaded into RAM and played back at different pitches. In addition samples can be seen as similar to the oscillators on an analogue synthesiser and further processed by filters, LFOs and ADSRs to modify the sound.

One of the problems with sampling is that, as you move the pitch away from the one the sample was originally sampled at, it can become 'munchkin like' as the pitch gets higher and 'slow and grainy' as the pitch reduces. While this may be good for some effects, it wouldn't help anyone trying to sample an accurate piano!

Info

The higher the sampling rate and the higher the bit depth means each sample takes up more disk space for storage. In the EXS24, it also means more RAM used and more CPU power taken to play back the sample.

Info

A CD rate, stereo sample, recorded at 44.1kHz, 16 bit will take up approximately 10MB per minute.

To get around this limitation, Many different pitches are sampled and spread across the MIDI range.

In Figure 14.5, several samples are spread across the keyboard range in an attempt to minimize the artefacts of transposing samples.

In an ideal world, a sample would be taken of each note. But the effort of matching each recording and the number of samples needed usually mean a compromise is made.

Figure 14.5

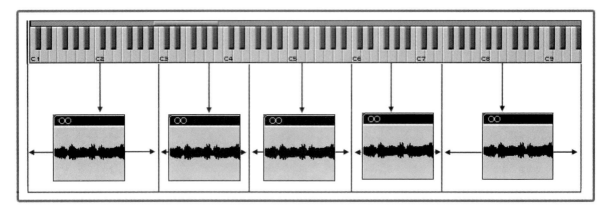

There is more on multi sampling in Chapter 15.

The EXS24 Sampler

T he EXS24 is a fully featured sampler, similar to hardware samplers such as the Akai series and EMU range. However, it has the following advantages.

- The more memory your computer has, the more samples you can store. Hardware samplers are often limited by RAM.
- You can run several EXS24s at once up to your CPU power limits.
- You can 'stream' samples from disk, effectively increasing the size of the samples the ESX24 can play back.
- All the modifying parameters (filters, envelopes etc) are available on screen all at once and can be automated.
- The EXS24 can load in samples from several popular sample libraries.

> **Info**
>
> The EXS24 cannot create samples on its own. You need to record a sound into Logic, edit the actual sample using the Audio editor and use that in the EXS24..

Sample organization

In EXS24 terminology, samples are the raw audio files that can be played back via the sampler. However the EXS24 doesn't just simply play back the raw samples. Samples are loaded into a Zone and these Zones are assigned to a Group. The Zones have parameters that affect the sample assigned to it. The Group has parameters that affect all the Zones assigned to that Group. Within this hierarchy, samples can be layered, spread across a keyboard and assigned to multiple outputs (Figure 15.1).

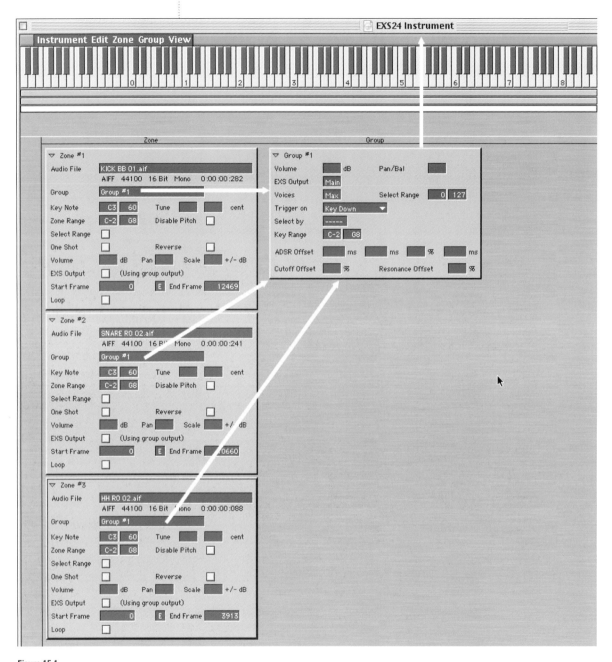

Figure 15.1
The EXS24 Sampler

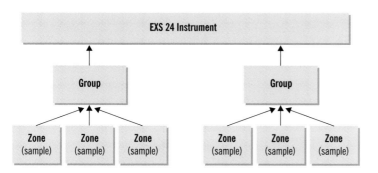

Figure 15.2
Hierarchy of the different parts making up an EXS24 Instrument.

The EXS24 Instrument is what you load into the ESX24. For example, the EXS 808 sound that comes with the sampler has many different drum samples residing in it spread across the keyboard.

Figure 15.3 (below)
Drum samples.

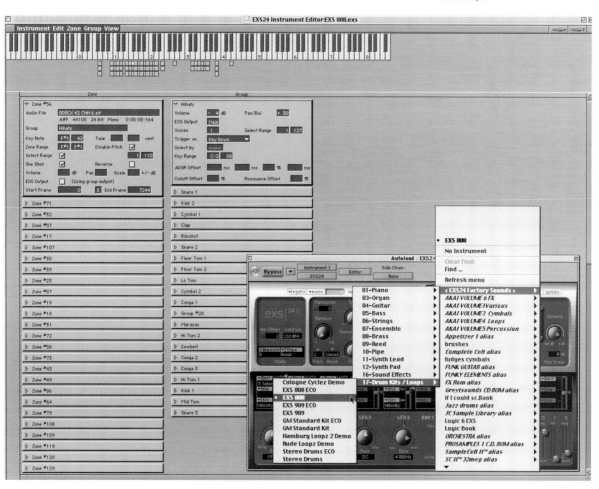

Figure 15.4
All the sampler's Instruments used by the EXS24 must reside in the Sampler Instruments folder within the Logic folder..

All the sampler Instruments used by the EXS24 must reside in the Sampler Instruments folder within the Logic Audio folder. However, you can have aliases to the real location of the EXS Sample Instruments themselves, so you can store them on any hard drive or CD. The EXS instruments are then available in the EXS24 pull down menu.

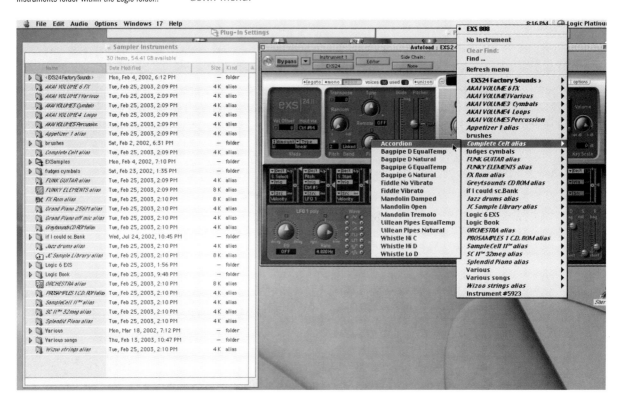

If you have a sample disc, such as Emagic Extreme beats or one of the Akai sample libraries, copy it to the hard disk. Then make an alias of the disc and copy that to the Sampler Instruments folder. Samples can reside in sub folders.

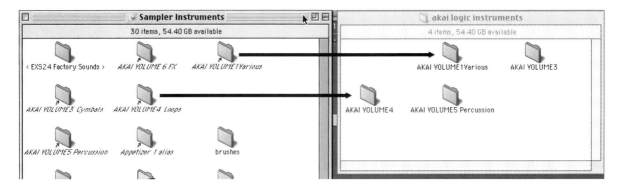

Loading EXS24 sampler sounds

It's likely that you have purchased sample disks in the EXS, AKAI, SampleCell, SoundFont, DLS or GIGA format and you'll want to use these sounds right away. Here's how to do it.

Make sure you have aliases to the samples residing in the Sampler Instruments folder as described above or the actual EXS Instruments themselves.

Select an EXS Instrument from the pull down menu. Play the keyboard or MIDI controller.

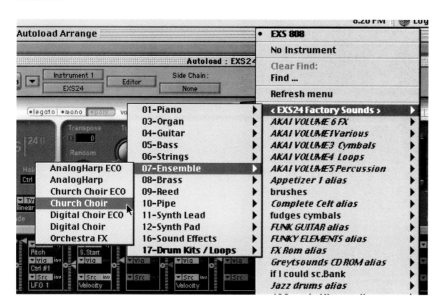

You can also use the + and – buttons to step through the EXS instruments.

Info

The samples themselves can be stored anywhere as long as they are on line when you load an EXS Instrument.

Info

When using other sample disks than 'native' EXS24 ones, some parameters may not translate correctly. Use the EXS24 format ones if possible.

Info

Because the EXS24 is loading samples from hard disk, changing sounds is not instantaneous!

Tip

Set up a Key command within Logic to change EXS sounds.

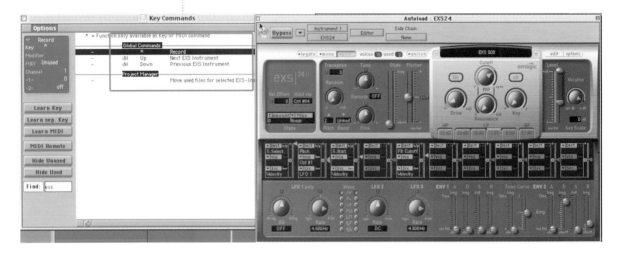

An EXS24 overall view

As you can see, the Plug-in window of the EXS24, like the ES2, looks complicated at first. But if we break it down into sections again, it'll make a lot more sense. In some respects, the ESX24 is a synthesiser that, instead of oscillators, has samples as the tone generation source.

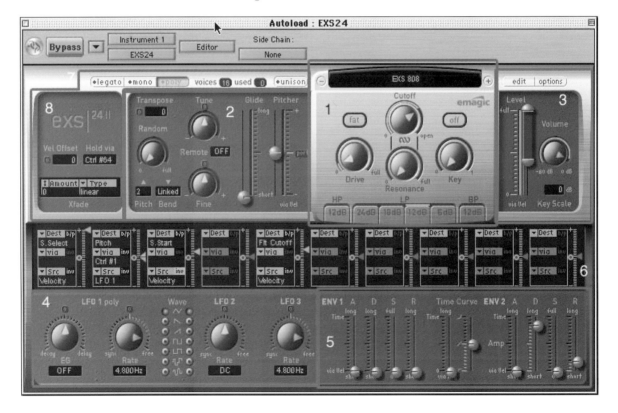

Section 1– Patch loader and Filter
Section 2 – The master tuning section
Section 3 – The output level. Instrument editor and Options menu.
Section 4 – Low frequency oscillators (LFO)
Section 5 – Envelope generators
Section 6 – The Router
Section 7 – Polyphony
Section 8 – Miscellaneous functions

First we'll look at the Plug-in window's parameters, then the details of Sampling using the ESX24.

Section 1 – Patch loader and Filter

The patch loader was discussed earlier in the chapter. The Filter is pretty standard apart from the following features.

   The filter is switched On and OFF using the button.

   You can modify the Cutoff and Frequency together by clicking and dragging on the chain symbol (right). Dragging horizontally affects the Resonance, vertically the Cutoff and both together when dragging diagonally.

   The drive control (below left) overdrives the input to the filter adding harmonics. The Moog filter is famous for having this feature.

   The Fat button (centre) maintains loss of bass as the resonance level increases. The Key knob (right) determines the relationship of the Filter Cutoff frequency to the note number. When the control is at 0, the Cutoff is not affected by note number – so the Cutoff stays the same as you play up the keyboard. When the control is at 1, the Cutoff frequency is progressively reduced as you play up the keyboard, reducing the brightness of higher notes and mimicking the behaviour of acoustic instruments. There is a variable range in between.

Filter types

There are four Low Pass (LP) slopes 6, 12, 18 and 24 dB per octave.
One High pass filter (HP) with a 12 dB slope.
One Band pass filter (BP) with a 12 db slope.

Section 2 – The master tuning section

Transpose sets the overall pitch of the EXS24 in semitones. This also affects the Zones transpose setting.

Tune – allows you to tune samples to bring them to the correct pitch. Tune is the coarse tuning in semitones, Fine is in cents (100th of a Semitone).

Remote – This parameter allows you to pitch complete EXS24 instruments in real time. Set the remote parameter to the key on your MIDI keyboard that was the 'original pitch' of the sample. Now, the EXS24 sets a plus and minus one octave range around this pitch.

Random – this acts like the Analogue control on other E-Magic Virtual instruments. It creates a random detune that attempts to simulate hardware analogue synthesisers.

Glide and Pitcher – When the Pitcher is set to the centre point, the Glide control acts in the normal way – i.e. it sets the time it takes for one note to slide to another.

When the Pitcher is set above the centre point, it acts as a pitch envelope. The pitch will fall from the Pitcher setting to the original value. The rate of the fall being determined by the Glide control.

When the Pitcher is set below the centre point, it acts as a pitch envelope. The pitch will rise from the Pitcher setting to the original value. The rate of the rise being determined by the Glide control.

When the slider is split, low velocity values will cause the pitch to rise to the centre value. With higher velocity values, the pitch will fall to the centre value.

Tip

You can drag the split slider up and down by clicking and holding on the bar between the controls and dragging.

Pitch bend – The left hand window sets the number of semitones of transpose the EXS24 produces when using the pitch bend wheel to bend up. A pull down menu appears when you click and hold on the window. The right hand window

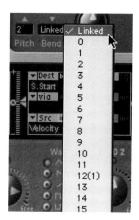

is used to set the range when moving the pitch bend wheel down. You can choose semitone steps or 'linked' which sets the same range as the pitch bend up parameter.

Section 3 – The output level, Instrument editor and Options menu

Level via Vel – this has a split slider. When the controls are together, the EXS24 doesn't respond to velocity. When it's split, the lower control sets the volume at the lowest velocity input, the upper control the volume at the highest velocity input.

Volume – this knob sets the overall level of the EXS24 output.

Key scale – if this is set to negative values, notes get quieter as you play up the keyboard. If it's set to positive values, notes get louder as you play up the keyboard. Its purpose is to maintain a constant volume over the whole MIDI note range, or to simulate instruments that get quieter or louder the higher the pitch.

The Edit button opens the instrument editor. More on this later.

The options button opens a pull down menu, allowing you to set some EXS Instrument settings.

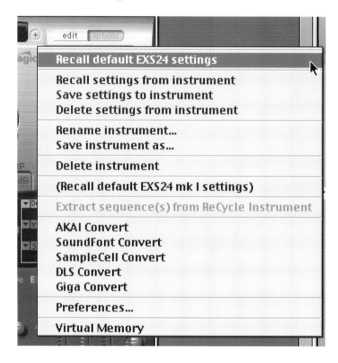

Recall default EXS24 settings – use this as the starting point for new EXS24 instruments.
Recall settings from instrument – resets the plug-in parameters to the instrument saved on disk.
Save settings to instrument – saves the plug-in parameters to the instrument overwriting the ones on disk.
Delete settings from instrument – deletes the plug-in parameters from the current Instrument.
Rename Instrument – change the name of the Instrument. The change will be visible in the patch pull down menu.
Delete instrument – deletes the current instrument.
Recall default EXS24 mk 1 settings – creates Router set-ups mimicking the hardwired set-ups of the MK 1 EXS24. The EXS24 Mk II has no fixed routing settings.
Extract sequence(s) from ReCycle Instruments – if you have any ReCycle instruments, you can extract the sequences contained therein and assign them to an EXS24 Instrument. More on this later.
Conversion types – here you'll find a list of the Sampler Instruments that EXS24 can use. More on this later.

Preferences – this opens a window (Figure 15.5) containing some EXS preferences.

SR Conversion – this sets the quality of the EXS sample rate conversion when you transpose a sample by playing up and down then keyboard. 'Best' uses the most CPU power.
Sample storage – this has two settings.
Original – EXS24 handles the samples in their original bit depth and converts them to 32 bit on loading.
32 bit Float – the samples are pre-stored in 32 bit depth for more efficient handling thus allowing higher polyphony. However, you'll need more RAM for these samples. 50 % more is needed than for 16 bit, 30% more than for 24 bit.
Velocity curve – this adjusts the overall response of the EXS24 to your MIDI keyboard. Negative values increasing the sensitivity to softer key hits.
Akai Convert thru – if the sample disks being converted are in the computers own CDROM use the operating system setting. If the CDROM is connected via a SCSI interface, choose it here.

Figure 15.5
The Preferences window.

Search samples on – choose the disks where EXS24 should search for samples.
EXS24 TDM mode – this deals with the Use of EXS24 with DigiDesign's TDM ProTools system through E-Magic's ESB bridge. You can run ProTools hardware alongside 'native' audio and route the EXS through the DigiDesign interfaces.
Read key note from – the Key note for the sample (i.e. the note it was originally sampled at), can be read from the file itself, the filename or a combination of both.
Key note at filename pos – selects where in the filename the information about the Key note is contained. Leave this at Auto.
Previous Instrument –
Next Instrument –

You can use a MIDI controller to change EXS24 Instruments. Set the controller and MIDI note number here.

Section 4 – low frequency oscillators (LFO)

The EXS24 has three LFOs. The destination of these is set in the Router.

LFO 1 and 2 have rate controls and a series of selectable waveforms. If the rate control is turned to the right, the LFO frequency is 'as set' by the control. If it's turned to the left, the rate can be synchronised to the tempo of the song. *LFO 1* is polyphonic, i.e. each voice played has it's own LFO, while LFO 2 and 3 are shared by all the voices.

LFO 1 has an Envelope generator (EG). When this is turned to the right LFO 1 will fade in, i.e. it becomes a delayed modulation. If it's turned to the left, the LFO modulation is faded out.

LFO 3 only has a rate control. It generates a triangle wave only.

Section 5 – Envelope generators

The ESX24 has 2 Envelope generators (EG).

The EXS24 has two identical ADSR type EGs. Which part of the EXS24 they affect is controlled by the Router.

Time curve – This extra parameter allows the envelopes of EG1 and 2 to be shortened as you play higher keys. Again, this is an attempt to simulate the characteristics of acoustic instruments. The Time slider sets this, while the Curve slider sets the slope of this effect, i.e. the speed of the shortening.

Section 6 – the Router

The Router is similar to the one in the ES2 synthesiser. It allows any modulation sources to control any destination. You can also route these set-ups through a third – a Via.

You could, for example, have a LFO controlling the pitch to produce Vibrato via the Modulation Wheel on your MIDI Keyboards. Up to ten Router units can be set up.

A – Source – clicking and holding on the Src (Source) parameter sets the part of the EXS24 that is doing the modulation. For example, the source could be an LFO.

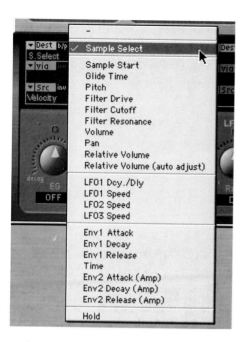

B – Destination – clicking and holding on the Dest (Destination) parameter sets the part of the EXS24 that is being modulated.. For example, the destination could be the Filter Cutoff producing a wha effect.

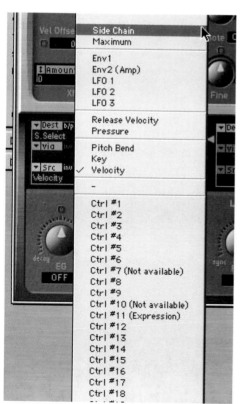

C – Via – you can insert another modulation source in between the Source and Destination. You could, for example insert a Modulation Wheel to control the wah effect.

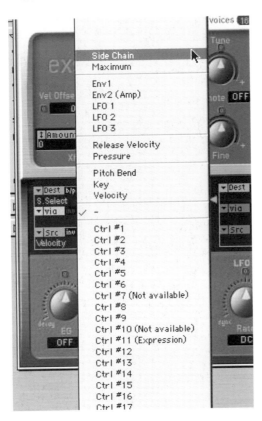

D – Intensity – the triangular controls at the side of the Router unit set the intensity of the modulation. You can set positive and negative values. If you insert a Via, the triangle splits in two. Dragging the dual slider up from the centre increases the intensity. Dragging it downwards, creates a negative intensity. If the slider is split, this sets the range of the modulation depth – i.e. in our example, the lower control would set the modulation intensity when the wheel is fully down, the upper control sets the intensity when the wheel is fully up.

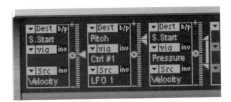

As you can see from the pull down menus, many different destinations can be modulated by many different sources. This makes the EXS24 a powerful synthesiser as well as a sampler.

The byp button on each router block bypasses the block. The inv button inverts the effect.

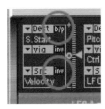

Importing other sample formats.

The EXS24 can import many other sampler formats, such as AKAI and GIGA. In most cases, just opening the sample instruments as if they were in EXS native format. A small window opens to show the conversion occurring. This method loads the entire Instrument and it can be used as if the non-native format was an EXS24 native Instrument.

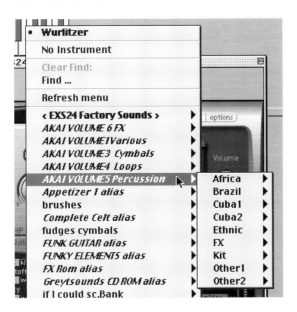

EXS24 will also import ReCycle Instruments directly. Importing separate samples from non-native CD formats can be done in the EXS24 Instrument editor.

Section 7 – polyphony

The EXS can play in the following modes:

Legato – this is a monophonic mode where Glide and the Envelope Generators are only retriggered when you release a previous note before playing a new one.

Mono – In this mode, the Glide and ENV generators are retriggered whenever a new note is played even if the previous note is not released.

Poly – This allows you to play more than one note simultaneously. The actual number you can play is set in the Voices parameter box.

The Used box shows the number of voices actually being used.

Unison – this parameter has different effects depending on the polyphony setting.

In Poly mode the EXS24 plays two voices per note. In Mono or Legato mode, each key pressed plays up to eight voices – the value being set in the Voices box. They are randomly detuned and spread over the stereo field using the Random knob.

Info

You can also set the polyphony of individual Groups in the Instrument editor.

Info

The more EXS24 voices playing, the more CPU power is used.

Section 8 – miscellaneous functions

Vel offset – this sets a Velocity offset for the whole Instrument loaded into the EXS24. If you have set a range of velocity response to, say, 12 to 120, setting this parameter to + 5 will move the range to 17 to 125. You can also input negative numbers to reduce the values.

Hold Via – This sets the MIDI Controller number that holds all currently playing notes. The default is 64 – the Sustain pedal.

Xfade (Crossfade) – these parameters allow you to crossfade the samples set up for Velocity switching as discussed in the practical examples later in this chapter.

Amount – this sets the range of velocity values that are crossfaded.

Type – sets the crossfade slope.

Using the EXS24 sampler

We'll use some real life examples to show how the EXS24 is used to create Sample Instruments.

Let's first create a 'Default' Instrument. First select 'Recall default EXS settings' from the options pull down menu.

Now select 'No Instrument' from the patch change menu.

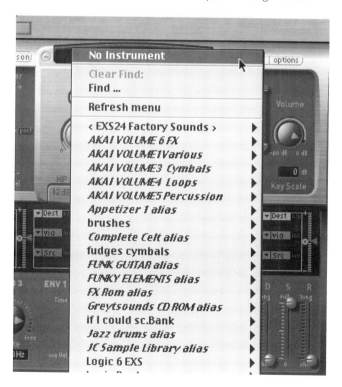

Click on the edit button on the plug-in. The Instrument editor opens. Select Instrument>New from the menu.

Select Instrument>Save As. Save the Instrument in the Sampler Instruments folder within the Logic Audio folder. It's called 'Logic Default' in this example.

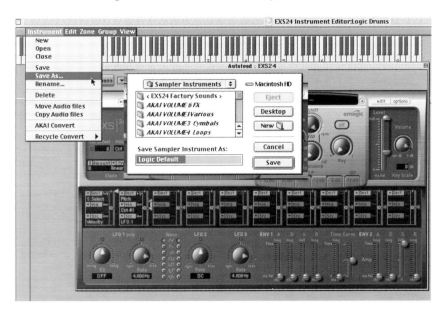

Now select it in the Instrument menu. If it's not there, select Refresh. This re-scans the Sample Instrument folder.

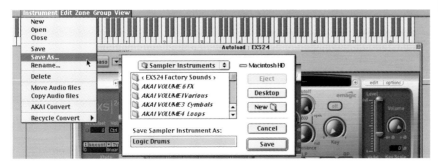

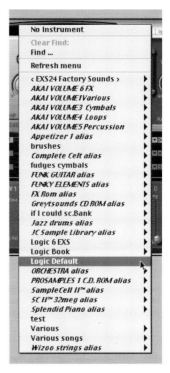

Use this default instrument to create the EXS Instruments shown on the right.

Creating a Drum kit instrument

For this, we are going to use the Multiple output (Multi Channel) version of the EXS24.

This will allow you to send different drum sounds to separate audio objects within Logic Audio for individual processing. More on this later.

You'll need a set of samples of Bass drum, Snare drum, hi hat open, hi hat closed and so on. It's convenient if these are all in the same folder.

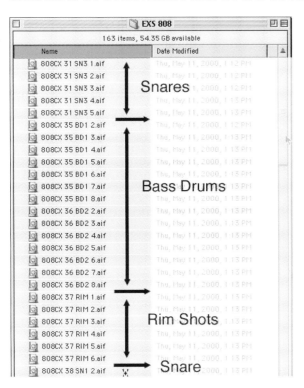

Info

The multiple output version of the EXS24 takes up slightly more CPU power than the 'regular' version.

Info

You can swap between Stereo and Multi Channel versions of the EXS24 on the same Instrument object at will. The settings will remain the same.

Now open the Instrument editor by clicking on the edit button (left). Make sure all the View menu items are selected.

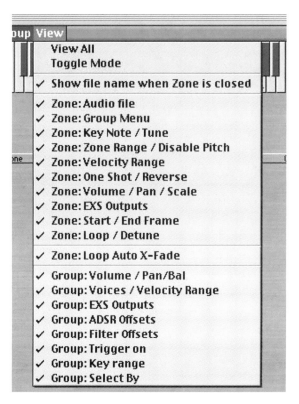

Select New Group from the Group menu. A Group box is opened. Rename it 'Hi hats' by double clicking on the Group name.

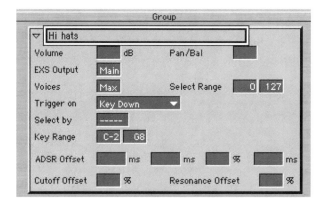

Select New Zone from the Zone menu.

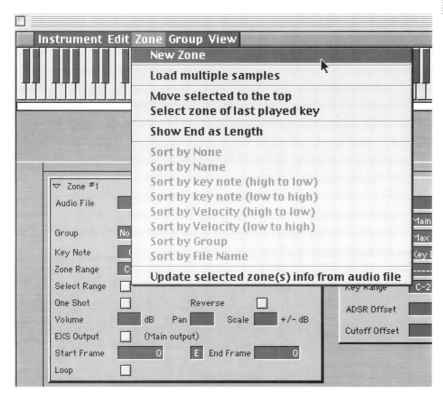

Click on the box to the right of Audio file on the Zone. A file selector opens. Select the Closed hi hat sample.

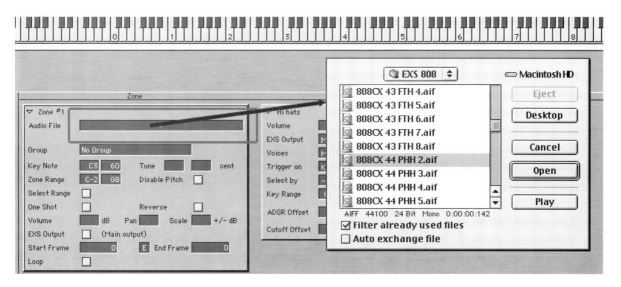

Click on the box to the right of Group and select 'Hi Hats' from the pull down menu. This assigns it to the Hi hats Group. Rename the Zone to 'Closed Hi Hat' by double clicking on the Zone name.

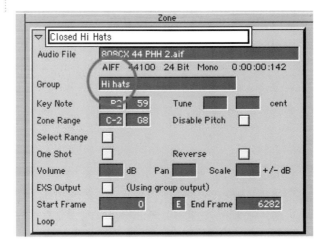

Now select New Zone from the Zone menu again. Note that the Zone 1 image collapses to a rectangle. You can open the Zone again by clicking on the little arrow at the top left of the rectangle.

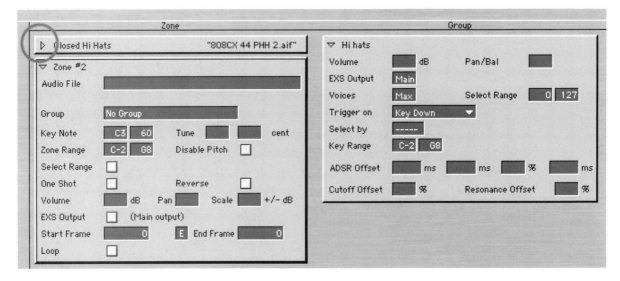

Load the Open hi hat sample in the same fashion as the first. Rename the Zone as before (Figure 15.6). Set the second Zone to the hi hats Group in the same fashion as for Zone 1 (Figure 15.7).

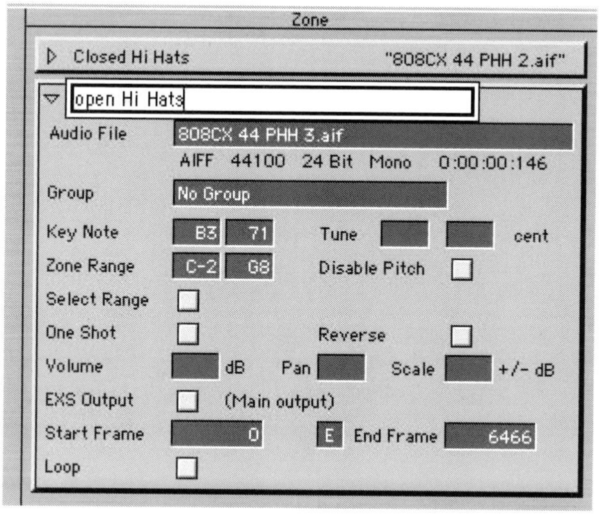

Figure 15.6

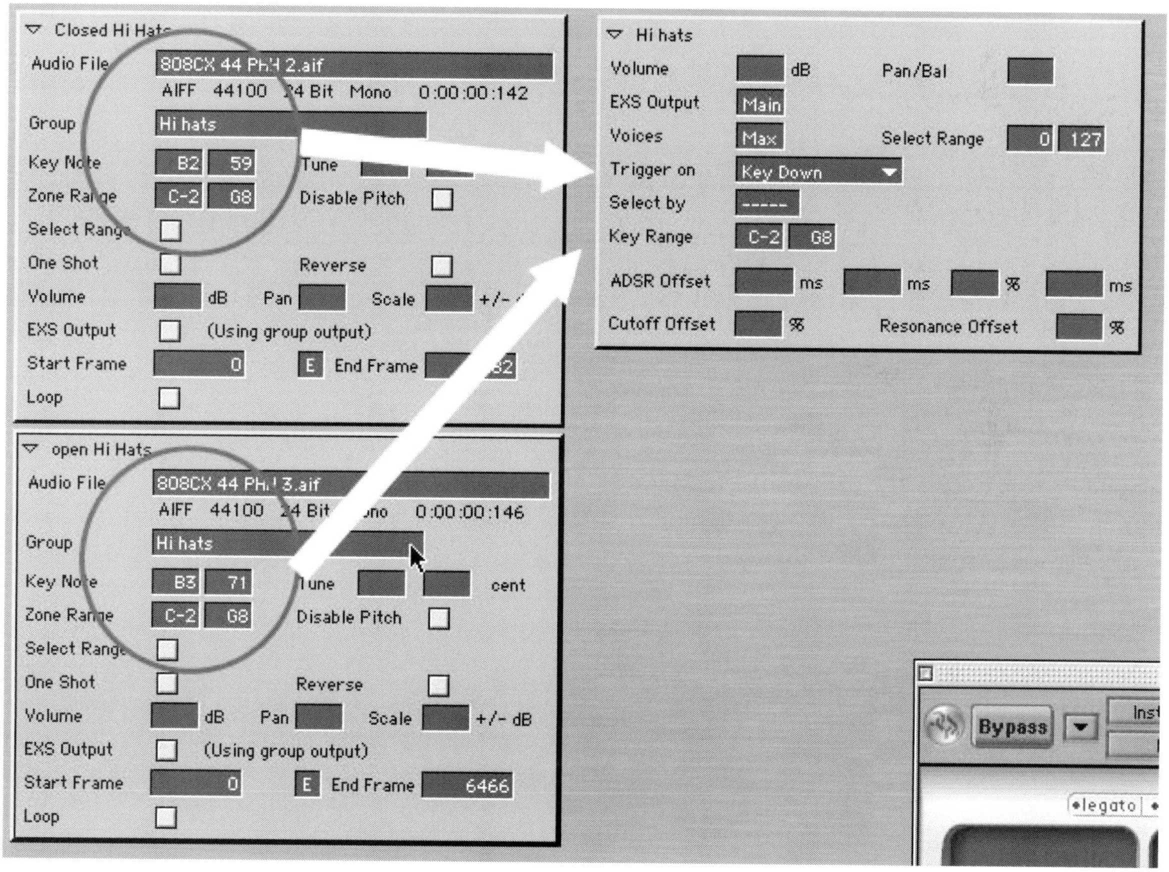

Figure 15.7

Create a new group using the Group>New Group menu item in the same fashion as for Group 1. Rename it to 'Snares'. Create another Zone. This time load in a snare sample. Rename the Zone as before.

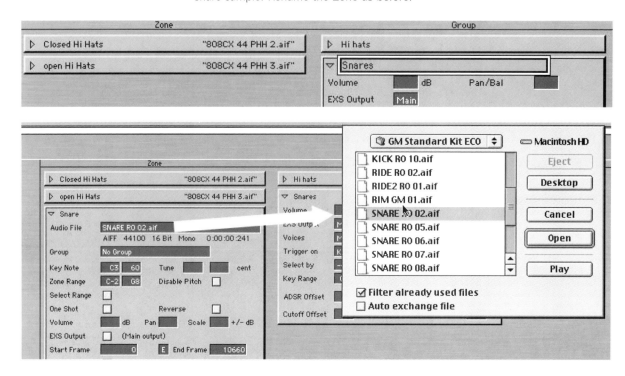

Chose the 'Snares' group for this Zone.

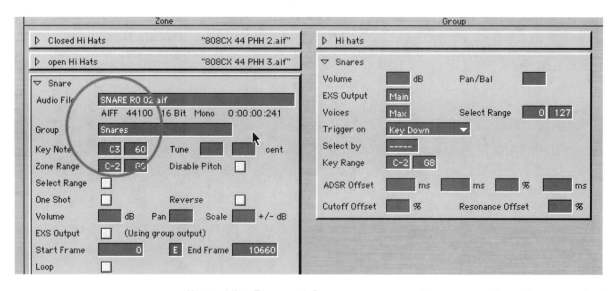

Keep adding Zones and Groups as necessary. You may want to add groups called 'Toms', 'Claps', 'Bass drums' and so on. Assign the Zones to the relevant groups.

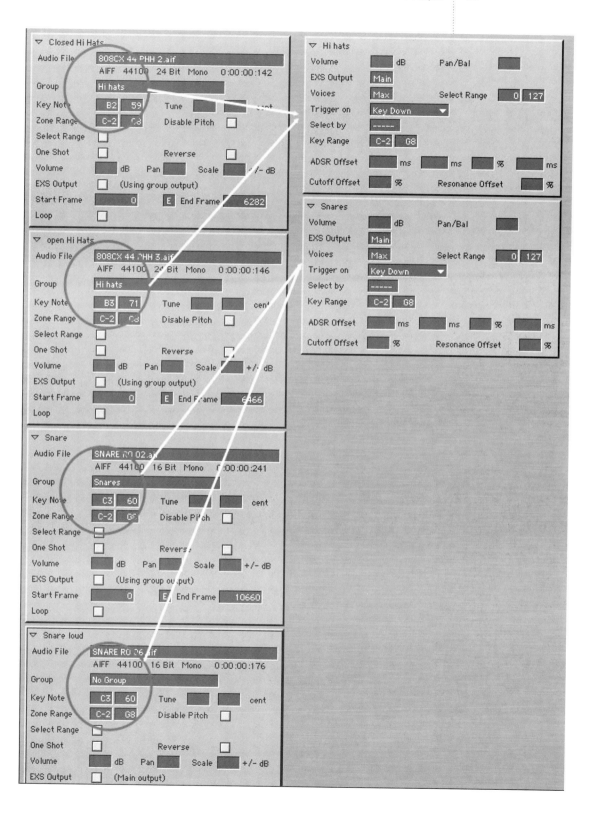

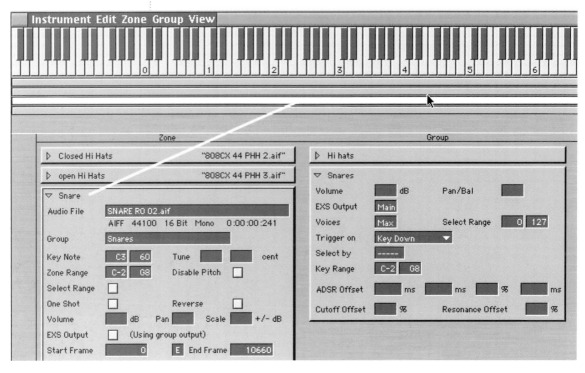

Now look at the top of the Instrument editor window. You'll see a representation of the Keyboard range with grey bars running underneath. These bars represent the Zones. If you click on a Zone the relevant bar is selected and vice versa.

As you can see, all the Zones are set to play over the entire range of the keyboard. For a drum kit, we'd prefer a single key or small range of keys to play each Zone. You set the key range using the Zone's Zone range parameters. The left box sets the lower key the Zone will play over, the Right on the Upper.

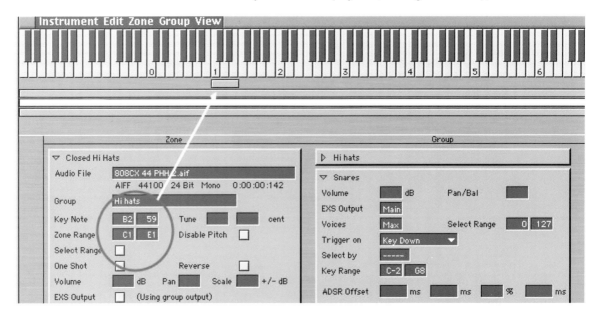

You can see that Zone 1, 'closed hi hat', now plays from C1 to E1 only.

Do the same with Zone 2, 'open hi hat', except make it play from F1 to A1,. Notice that now the range butts up against Zone 1 – the Zone has moved up next to Zone 1.

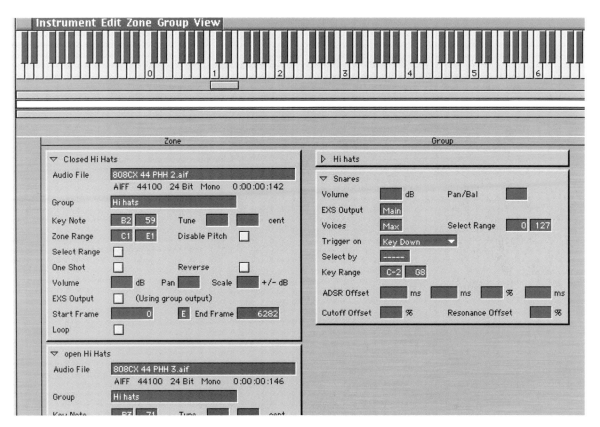

Repeat this for all the Zones. Note that they are all now butted up together.

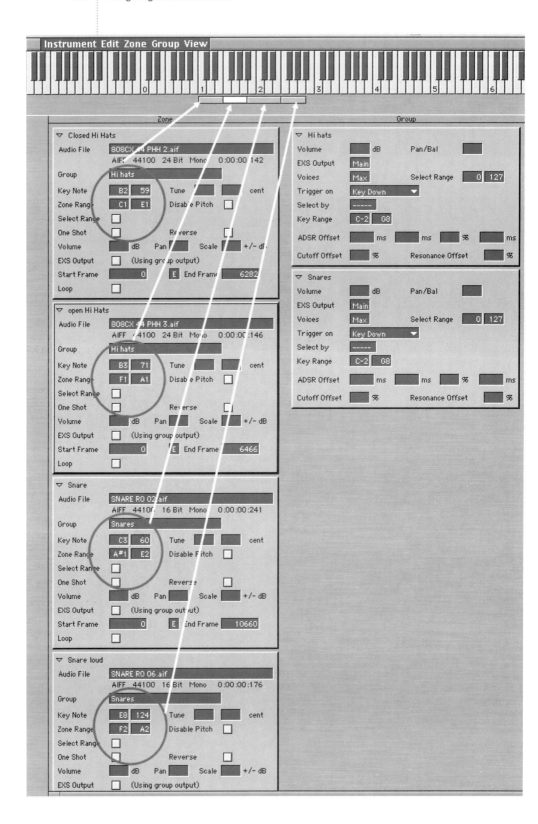

As we want all the notes ranged by a given sound to be the same pitch no matter which key is pressed, make sure the 'Disable Pitch' box is checked on each Zone.

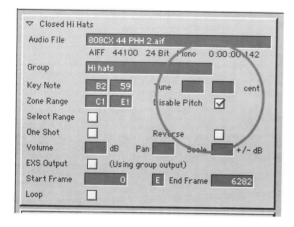

Add as many samples as you need.

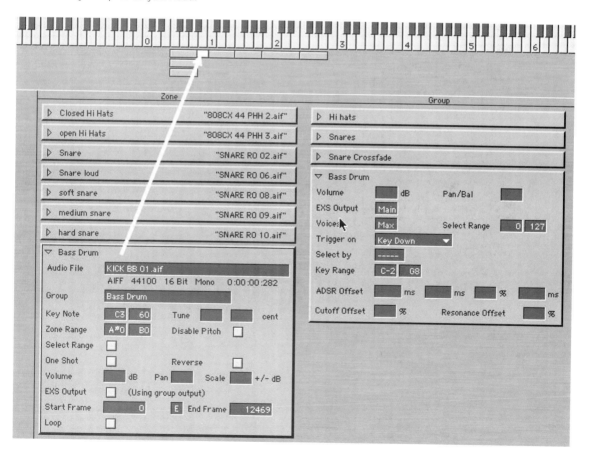

Save the Instrument into the Logic Audio Sampler Instruments folder. If you save it somewhere else, you'll have to make an alias and copy that into the Sampler Instruments folder.

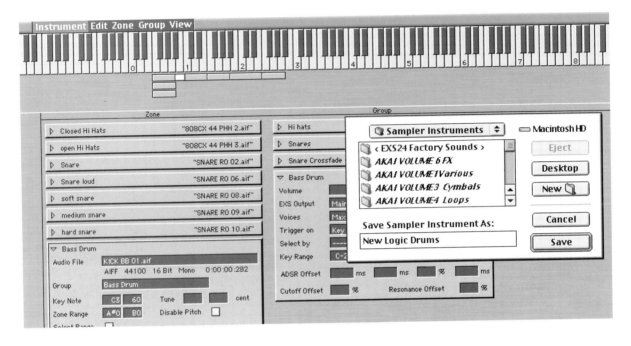

As you can imagine, it's a pretty dull drum kit! There are various ways to improve it.

Making the kit velocity sensitive

Making the drum sounds responsive to how hard you hit a key can make the sound more expressive. Here's how you do it.

Set the Level via vel. The top control sets the level of the output when maximum velocity is input from a keyboard (127). The lower control sets the level at the minimum velocity (0).

Velocity crossfading

When you hit a drum quietly, it sounds completely different to the same drum struck harder. To increase the realism of a drum sound, we could record drums at different volume levels and then used the velocity of the incoming MIDI data to switch between the samples.

Say we recorded a snare drum hit quietly, medium and hard. Here's how you set this up in EXS24.

- Create a new Group. Call it 'Snare crossfade'.
- Create three new Zones. Rename them 'soft snare', 'medium snare' and 'hard snare'.
- Assign them to the Zone 'Snare Crossfade'
- Click the Disable pitch button on each Zone.
- Load the three samples into the three zones.

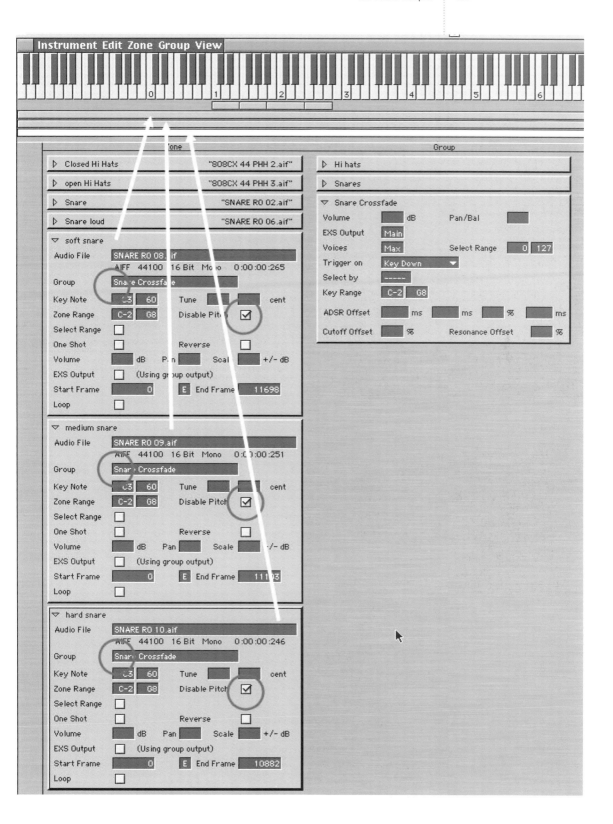

Give all three Zones the same zone range. Note that all the sounds are 'stacked'.

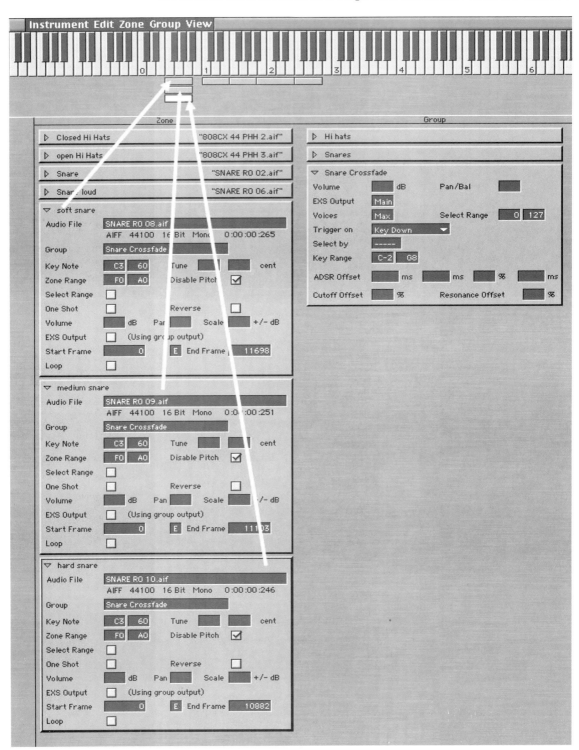

Now, click the Select range button on each zone and set the following values in the two windows that open to the right of the button.

Zone soft snare 0,40
Zone medium snare 41,100
Zone hard snare 101, 127

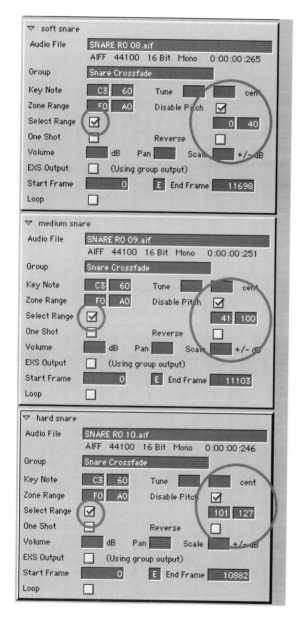

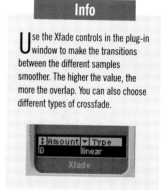

Now, when you hit a key lightly (velocity values 0 to 40), the soft snare sample will play. Slightly harder hits (41 to 100) and the medium snare sound will play. Hitting the key harder (101 to 127) plays the hard snare sample.

Using multiple outputs

In a drum machine or sampler, it's often useful to send the different drum sounds to different outputs so they can be processed and equalized separately. For example, you may want to send the snare through a reverb, EQ the bass drum separately and differently to the hi hats. You can do this with the ESX24 using the Multi Channel (multiple output) version.

You can either send whole Groups to different outputs or single samples. These are sent to Aux objects within Logic Audio.

Here's how to do it. Create a new Environment layer. Call it 'Aux'. From the New menu, create an Audio Object. Double click on it to enlarge the object. From the Cha parameter in the Parameter box Select Aux.

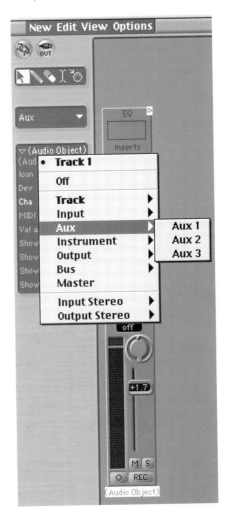

Repeat this to create another Aux object. Rename them Bass drum and Snare Drum.

Info

More Aux objects are created in the Cha parameter as new Auxes are created.

Insert the Multi Channel version of the EXS24 into an Instrument object.

Load in the new Logic Drums Instrument we created earlier.

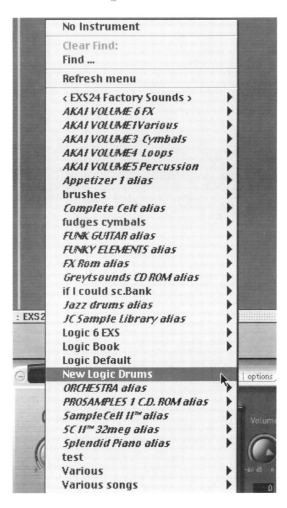

Now, let's send the Bass drums in the Bass Drums zone to the new Aux object.

Select the Bass Drum Zone in the Instrument editor. Click on the EXS output box. You'll see a pull down menu. Choose outputs 3 – 4. As the Bass Drum is a mono sample, you'll need to Pan the sound to the left, or –100 in the Pan box.

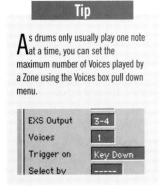

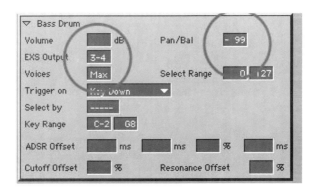

Now, click on the Input box of the Bass Drum Aux. You'll see an Instrument menu. Select EXS 24 3.

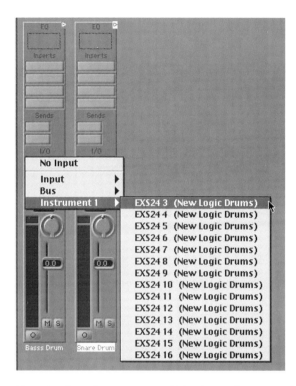

Now the Bass Drum sound will be heard from Aux 1, the Bass Drum Aux. The sound is also removed from the 'Main' Instrument object output.

You can now add compression and EQ to the Aux to process the Bass drum only (pic right).

Now let's send the Snares in the Snares Group to Aux 2. Select the Snares Group. Set the EXS output parameter to 5-6. As the Snares are stereo recordings, leave the Pan parameter blank.

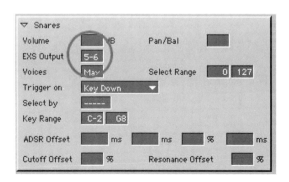

Now make Aux 2 a Stereo object by clicking on the Stereo button (pic left).
  Now click and hold on the Input box and select EXS 24 5-6 as inputs.

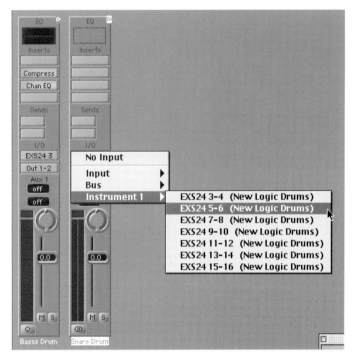

The Snare sounds are routed through Aux 2 and their outputs removed from the main Instrument object outputs. You can now add EQ. Compression and reverb just to the snare (left).

  Note that any sounds that are NOT sent to separate outputs still emerge from the main Instrument object that the EXS24 is Instanced on. You can use this as an extra output.

Creating a piano instrument

If you record a single note of an acoustic piano, say at middle C and load that sample into the EXS24, it will sound like a real piano when played at middle C. However, as you play up and down the keyboard, you'll notice some strange effects. The higher you play the shorter the sample will become and the higher in frequency. As you play lower, the sound will slow down and sound more like a piano played in some strange basement. While these effects can produce unusual sounds, they are not ideal when you're trying to get an accurate piano representation.

  The way around this problem is to use many samples of the piano spread across the keyboard. You could use 88 samples, one for every key on a piano, but this could cause problems as one note changes to another. It's more common to use one or two samples per octave.

  A piano is also a dynamic instrument. Softly played notes are completely different in tone to those played harder. So we'll want to record soft and hard piano samples too.

So, to summarise, these are the samples we'll need:

Piano played hard
Piano played soft

And the notes we'll use are

C0, G0
C1, G1
C2, G2
C3, G3
C4, G4
C5, G5
C6, G6

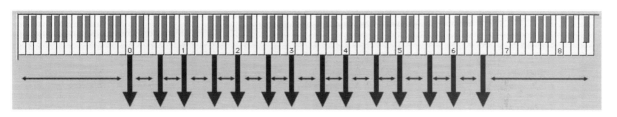

So, say we wanted to recreate a seven octave Piano with two samples per octave at two velocities, we'd need 14 x 2 or 28 samples.

Recording the samples

Make sure each strike is of a similar velocity and not too different in tone. The alternative is to use some of the many audio or audio file (WAV, AIFF etc) CD sample disks which are available free with music magazines or from retailers, to get your samples. You'll probably get better sounds that way unless you have access to wonderful microphones, a nice sounding room and a 100 year old Steinway Grand!

When recording the sample, hit the note and let it sustain to silence. Use the Logic Audio Sample editor to remove unwanted noises at the start and end of the sample. Record in stereo if possible.

Creating the Piano Instrument

Use the 'normal' Stereo version of the EXS24.

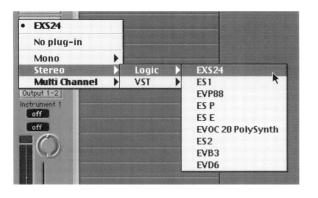

Select the Logic Default Instrument we made earlier.

To make the manipulation of the samples easier, we'll create two Groups for every octave, one for hard and one for soft, and assign the four samples per octave as Zones to these Groups.

Let's set up the first octave.

Open the Instrument editor by clicking on the edit button on the plug-in window. Create two Groups and four Zones. Rename them as necessary. Assign the
Zones to the relevant groups, i.e. C0 and G0 hard are assigned to the Octave 1
hard Group, G0 and G0 soft assigned to the Octave 1 soft Group. Load the relevant samples.

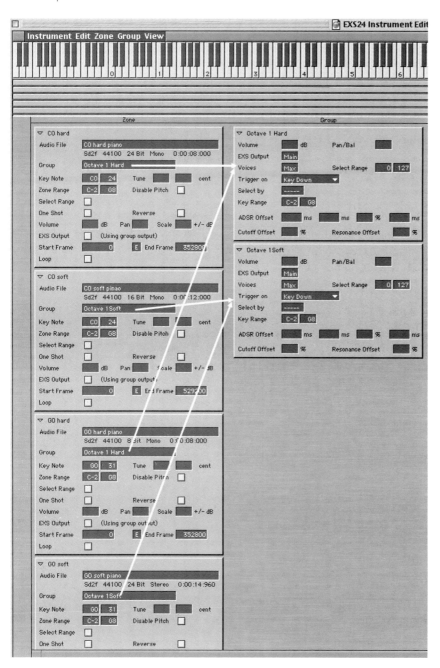

Continue until all Zones are loaded.

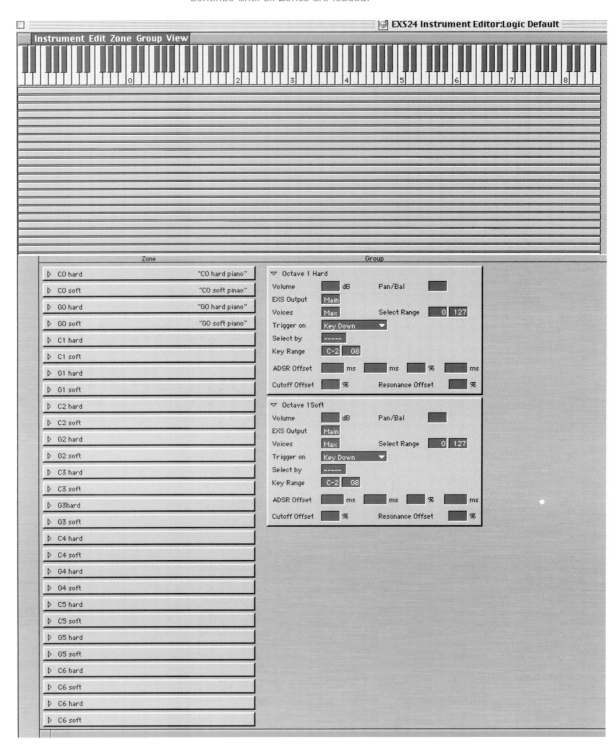

.

Now set the Zone ranges to the correct octaves and positions

Octave 1 C note hard and soft sample are set to C0 – F sharp 0
Octave 1 G note hard and soft sample are set to G – B 0

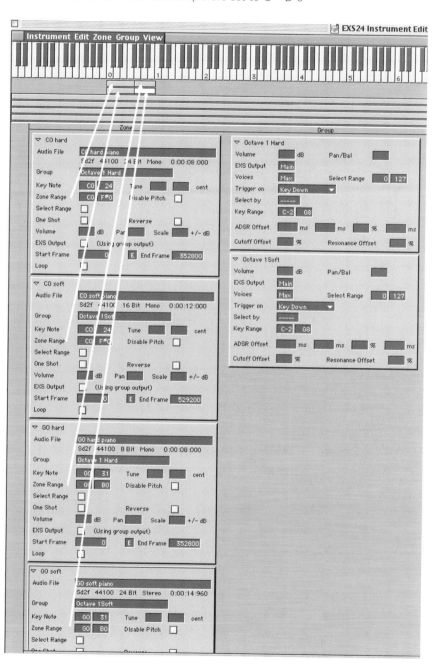

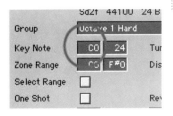

Now set the Key note for each zone to the note the sample was made at, i.e. C0 hard will be set to C0.

The value in the right hand box is the MIDI note value of the selected Key note (left).

This makes sure that the sample plays the correct pitch when you play the note it was originally recorded at.

Now repeat the previous section for every octave in the Piano.

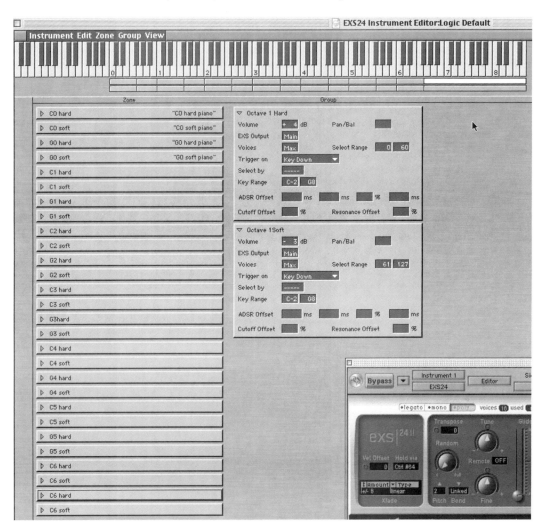

Now let's set the Velocity switch – how hard you need to hit the key before the hard piano is heard rather than the soft. This is usually done by ear. Initially try selecting a value of 0 – 160 for the soft Group, 61 to 127 for the hard one.

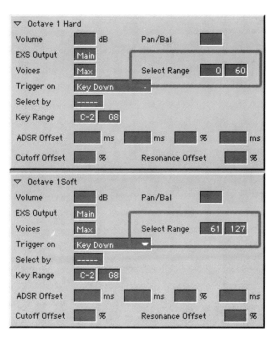

Try hitting the key until and changing the upper value of the Soft Group and lower value of the Hard Group until the changeover is in the right place.

You may find that the switch between the two samples is too obvious. There are several ways to alleviate this problem. If one of the two Groups is too loud, Change the Volume parameter.

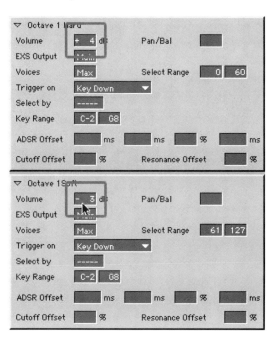

Try using the Xfade parameter in the plug-in window. This crossfades the soft and loud samples. Start with a value of 10. Try the different Types – these are the crossfade slopes.

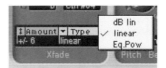

Try adjusting the Level via vel sliders to maximize the velocity range.

Change the Vel offset parameter to change the velocity sensitivity of the EXS24.

You may find that the transition between the Groups as you play up the keyboard is still too noticeable. You can try overlapping samples (see pic opposite).

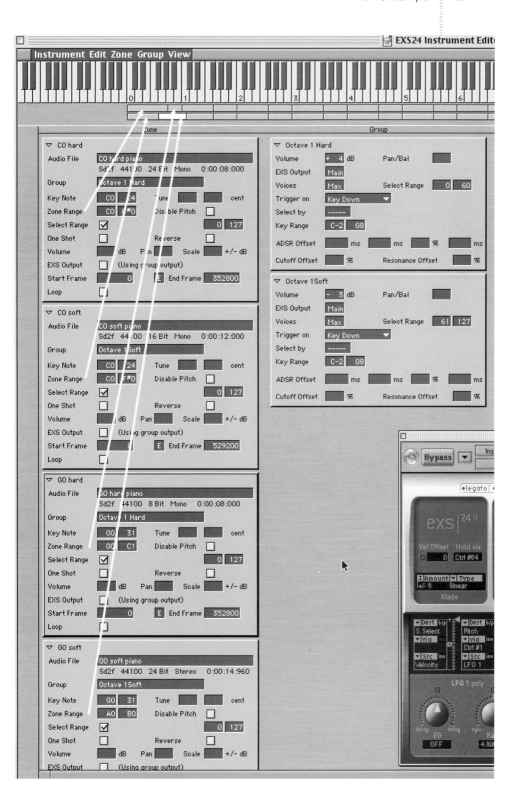

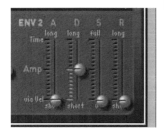

Now set the ENV 1 ADSR as in the figure on the left. This sets a 'piano like' volume envelope. Set the decay so that the piano sounds natural when pressing and holding a key.

Turn the Filter ON. Choose a Resonance and Cutoff value that makes the samples around Middle C (C3) sound right (below left).

Now, try adjusting the Cutoff and Filter offsets in the Groups. These add or subtract values from the plug-in Filter settings to make the sound brighter or softer.

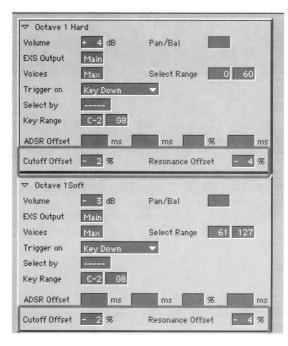

The Sustain pedal

To recreate the effect of the Sustain pedal on a real piano, you'll need to do the following. Connect a sustain pedal to your MIDI controller and make sure it sends out MIDI controller 64. Set the Hold via parameter to 64

Now, when you hold down the sustain pedal, each sample will play through to the end of the decay of the sound, even if you release the keys.

Making the sound more realistic

The Decay rate of a real piano note gets faster as you play up the keyboard. You can simulate this by adding a progressively more positive ADSR offset to the lower Groups and a negative offset to the higher Groups (Figure 15.7).

Try using the Key scale parameter to simulate the way a real piano gets quieter as you play up the keyboard. Select negative values to make the higher notes quieter (Figure 15.8).

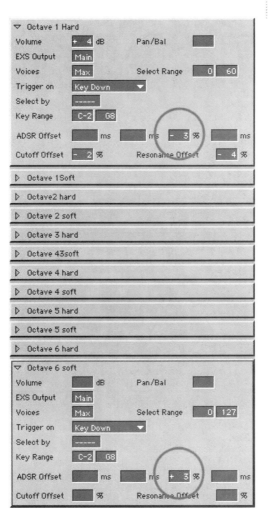

Figure 15.7
Add a progressively more positive ADSR offset to the lower Groups and a negative offset to the higher Groups.

Figure 15.8
Use the Key scale parameter to simulate the way a real piano gets quieter as you play up the keyboard.

Use the Key knob on the filter to change the Cutoff frequency as you play up the keyboard. Try modulating the Filter Cutoff by velocity. Set this up in the Router. Don't forget to save the Instrument under a new name!

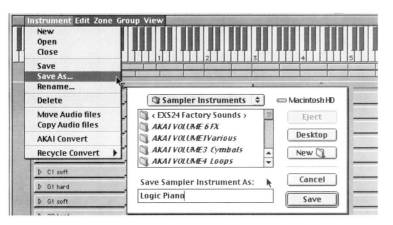

Creating synthetic instruments

As mentioned earlier, the EXS24 is a powerful synthesiser. But where are the oscillators? We can use samples as the oscillators. This has the advantage that the sound source could be a sample of a traditional waveform, such as a triangle or square wave, a sample of a 'classic' synthesiser or any sound at all.

The Piano and Drum Instruments described earlier used 'one-shot' samples – i.e. recordings of sounds that decay naturally to silence. To create a synthesiser sound, we need the samples to play for as long as the key is pressed. You'll also want to consider making multiple samples as for the Piano Instrument. You'll probably not need as many as for the Piano – four to six should be enough. Each sample should be a few seconds long.

* Load the Stereo EXS24 Logic Instrument.
* Load the Logic Default Instrument we created earlier.
* Open the Instrument editor by clicking on the edit button.
* Create a Group. Rename it 'Synth hi'. Create a Zone. Rename it 'hi synth sample'
* Load in the 'high synth' sample by clicking on the Audio file box. Assign it to the Group.

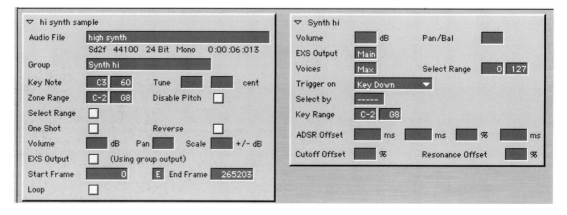

If you play the keyboard now, you'll hear the sample play its whole length through then stop.

The Start frame and End frame parameters are the first and last samples of the sample. You can edit it directly by clicking on the E. The Sample editor opens.

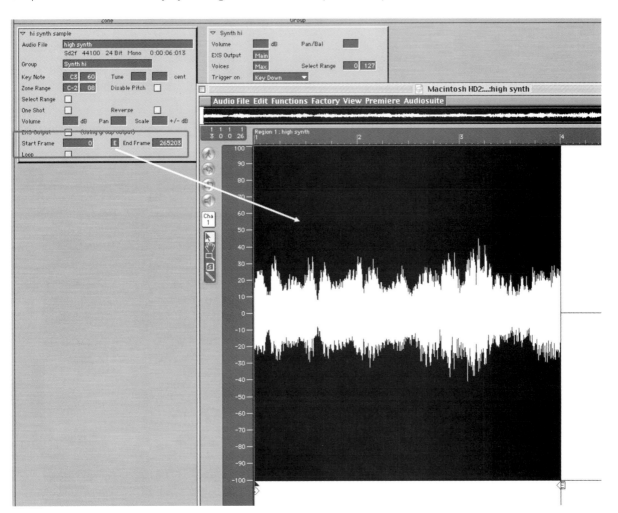

Looping the sample

Click on the Loop button. Two boxes will open up. These represent the Start and End frame of the loop. The sound will loop around these values. However, it's a lot easier to edit the Loop in the Logic audio sample editor. Set the Start to 10000 and the End to about 10000 samples less than the actual sample end. Click on the E. The sample editor opens. You'll see the Loop points.

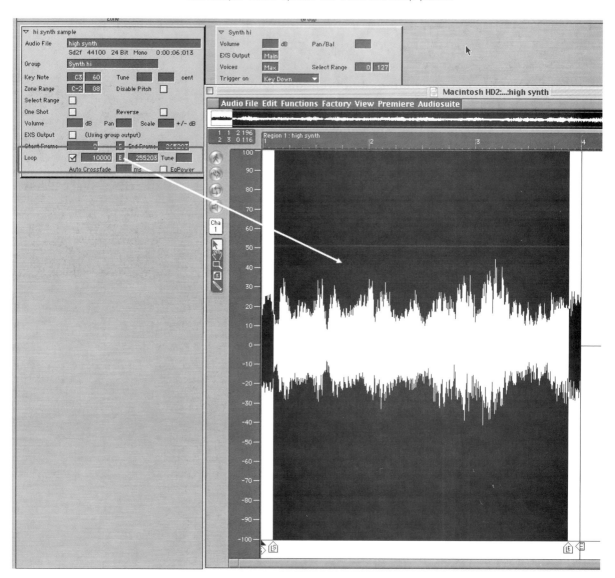

You can change the Loop start and End points using the Ls and Le cursors. Just drag them until the loop sounds smooth.

If you are having problems getting the loop to sound smooth at the start and end, try using the Auto crossfade parameter. EqPower can be used to compensate for the volume loss at the crossfade point.

Once you have a nice sounding loop, you can add more samples. Read the section on creating a Piano Instrument to see how to make sure the samples all sound OK when you play up the keyboard.

Finally save the Instrument

Now you have the 'oscillator' sound you can process it further using the plug-in window parameters.

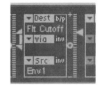

- Use the Filter to adjust the tonality of the sound. Create a Router block allowing the Cutoff to be modulated by ENV1 or the Mod wheel to produce wah (above right).
- Use ENV2 to create an amplitude envelope- change of the volume of the sound over time while a key is pressed (mid right).

- Set up a Router block to create vibrato by using LFO1 to modulate the pitch of the EXS24. Set up a Router block to use LFO 2 to modulate the Filter Cutoff (below right).
- If you have two different samples that play on the same key you can swap between them using Velocity or the Mod Wheel or any Controller by setting up Router blocks.
- Use the Xfade parameter to allow smooth crossfading between the samples.

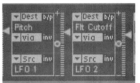

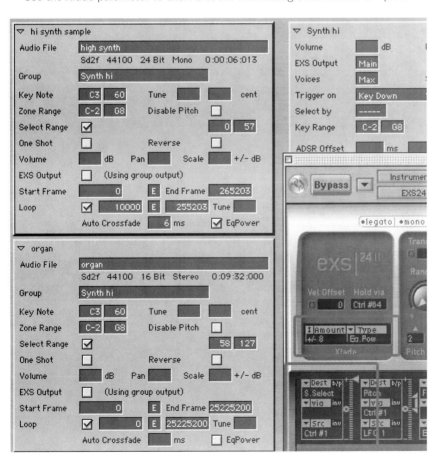

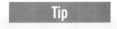

Tip

Use Logic Audio's Automation facility to record the crossfading to create pseudo wavetable synthesis.

Other useful EXS24 stuff

ReCycle import into the instrument editor

EXS24 has several items in the Instrument menu dealing with the loading of ReCycle Instruments.

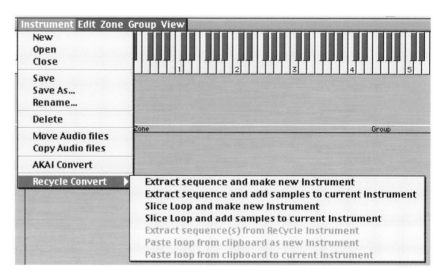

Extract sequence and make new instrument – this creates an EXS24 Instrument with the ReCycle slices spread across the keyboard. It also creates a MIDI sequence that will play back the original ReCycle loop.

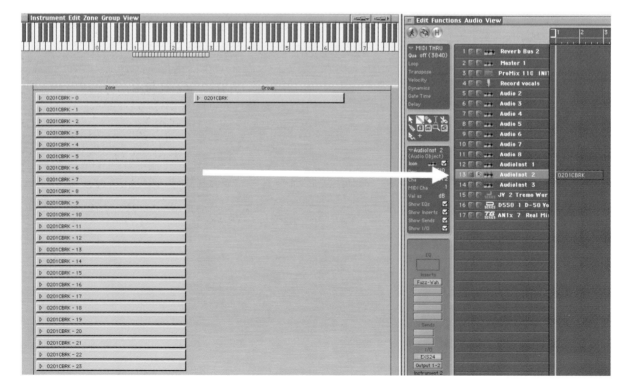

Extract sequence and add samples to current Instrument – same as above, except the samples are added to the current Instrument rather than creating a new one.

Slice Loop and make new Instrument – as Extract sequence and make new instrument but no sequence is created.

Slice Loop and add to current Instrument – as above, but the samples are added to the current Instrument.

Extract sequence(s) from ReCycle Instruments – extracts the MIDI sequence without the sample slices.

The remaining two menu items are used when a loop is placed in the clipboard when running ReCycle alongside Logic Audio. You can then paste the ReCycle loop into the EXS24.

Loading several samples at once into the Instrument editor

Selecting the Zone>Load multiple Samples menu item, opens up a window where you can select multiple samples.

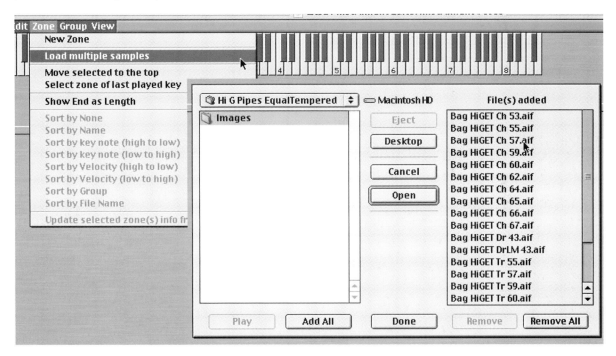

You can Add individual samples or all of them. Click on Done when you've got all the samples you want. A window opens with several options.

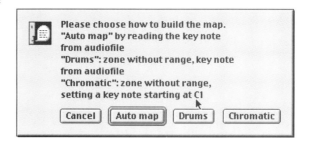

Auto map – reads the key note (i.e. the root note of the sample) from the file itself.
Drums – sets each new Zone to one key.
Chromatic – creates a Zone without range. The key note is set to C1.

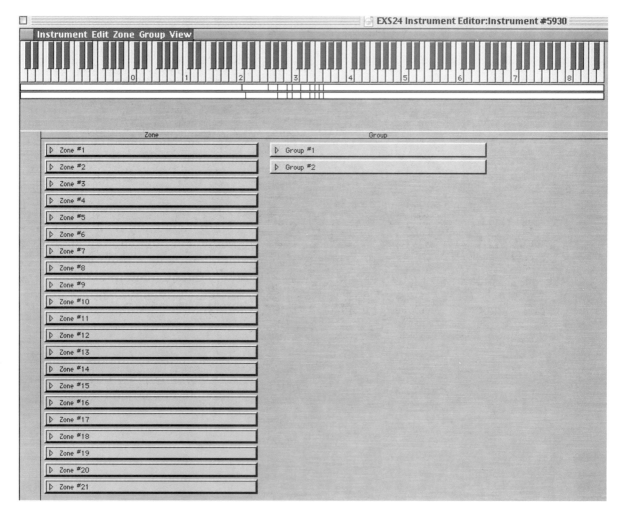

Akai Sample Importing

With Akai CDROMS you can choose to convert the whole CDROM by placing it in the Sampler Instruments folder as discussed earlier. You can also extract the Audio files (samples), Programs and other sample hierarchy separately. The AKAI convert window is opened from the Options menu or the Instrument editors File>AKAI convert menu.

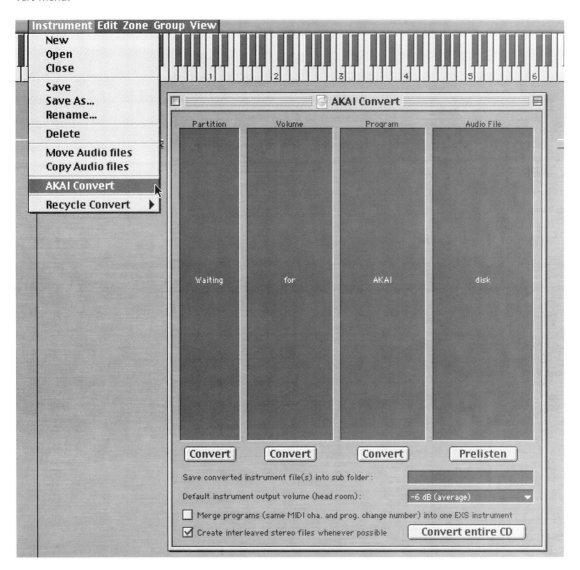

Virtual sample memory (VSM)

Usually, when you load a sample into the EXS24 it's stored in RAM and accessed from there when you play the sampler. This means that the number and size of samples that can be loaded is limited by the amount of RAM you have in your computer. VSM plays back samples directly from the hard drive, effectively allowing the EXS24 to use samples of any size. The disadvantage is that it will put a further strain on your hard drive when using it for audio file playback alongside the EXS24 – you may get less audio tracks.

Selecting VSM from the options menu opens up the following window.

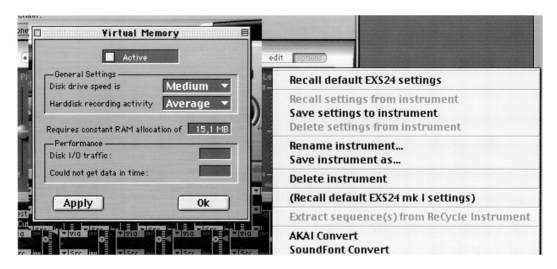

Active – activates the VSM
The General settings allow you to maximize performance depending on your hard drive.
The Performance windows show how well VSM is getting data off the disk.

Other EXS24 parameters

Search – you can search for samples using the Instrument selector pull down menu Find menu

Maximising CPU usage

V irtual Instruments use up a lot of CPU power. The more powerful the Instrument, the more CPU cycles used. If you use a lot of Virtual instruments in your song you can eat up CPU power rapidly.

You can keep your eye on the CPU usage using the CPU monitor. This can be opened by a Key command or the main menu item Audio>CPU monitor.

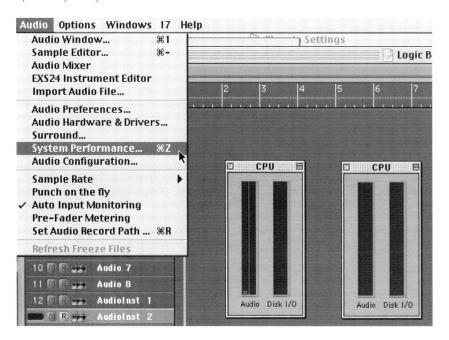

Logic 5 and earlier

You can free up CPU resources by bouncing the track to an Audio file. Here's how you do it.

Open an Arrange page, a Transport and the Track mixer and stack as follows. Make sure you have a master fader on the Arrange page. Select the Sequence the Virtual instrument is playing on.

Set the left and right locators to the beginning and end of the sequence. Turn on cycle mode.

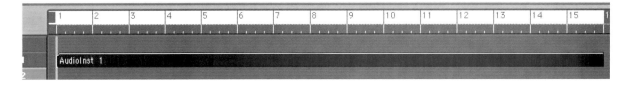

Click on the Bounce button on Master Audio object the Track mixer. The bounce dialogue window opens. The length of the bounce is shown in the window. Click on 'Bounce and Add'. Create a filename for the bounce.

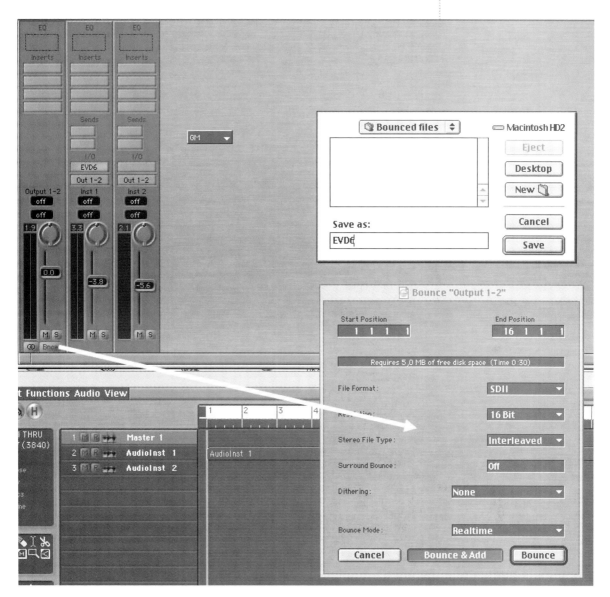

You will hear the Virtual instrument being recorded to disc. If you have any automation this will be recorded too. If you have any plug-in effects on the Virtual Instrument it's best to hold down the Option key and click on these to bypass them.

When the bounce is complete, create a new Audio Track and drag it next to the Virtual instrument track. Open the Audio window and locate the bounced file at the bottom of the window.

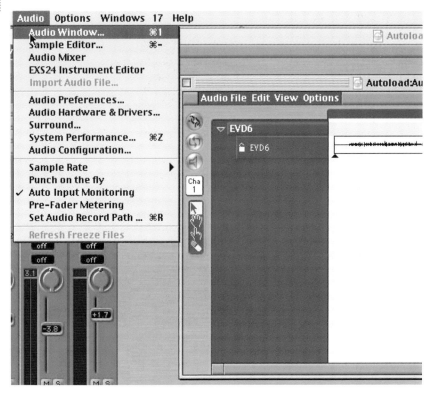

Drag the bounced file to the same place as the Virtual instrument sequence.

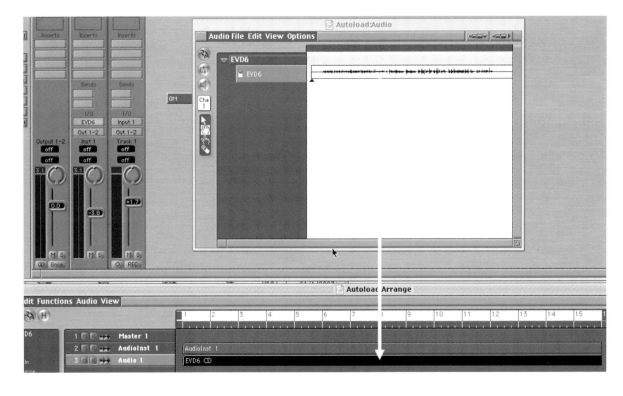

Mute the Virtual instrument track.

Bypassing the Virtual Instruments will save only a few CPU cycles. You really need to remove it from the song. Save the song as a backup. Call it something like 'Original Song with EVD6'. Reopen the original song. Open the Virtual instrument plug-in. Use the Save command to save the Instruments preset you are using.

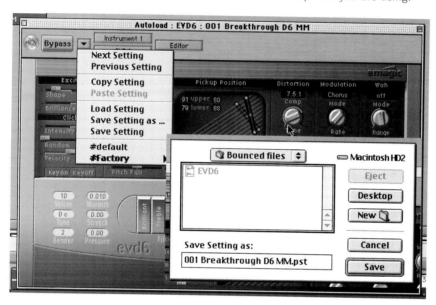

Remove the Virtual instrument.

Logic 6

There's a Freeze function in Logic 6 which renders the Instrument, along with any plug-ins and plug-in automation to an Audio file. The Instrument object is then automatically muted and the CPU resources released.

All plug-in parameters will be unavailable after a Freeze, but all automation will be written to the rendered file. However, you can still use and automate the following

• Volume, mute and solo
• Panorama and Surround values
• Effect send levels and their destinations

If you need to tweak a frozen track, just un-freeze it, edit, and then re-freeze it! You cannot cut the frozen tracks, nor move the sequences around. If you try to do an 'illegal' edit, Logic will ask if you want to un-Freeze the track. Here's a typical recording of an instrument (in this case the ES2) with effect plug-ins and automation.

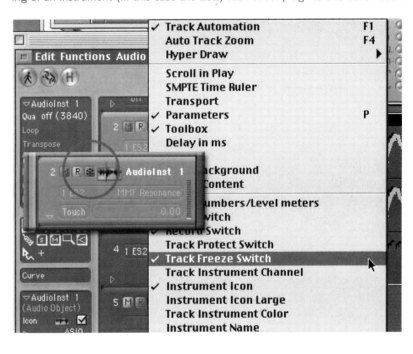

Make sure the Freeze icon is displayed using the Arrange page View>Track Freeze switch menu item is selected. A new icon appears in the instrument column.

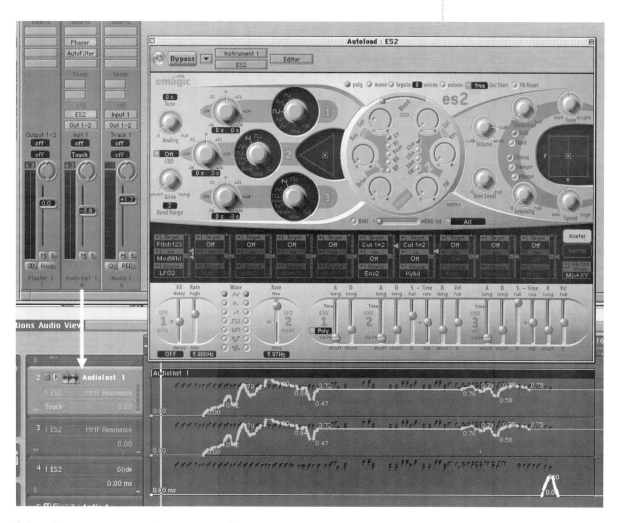

Select the sequence or track you want to Freeze.

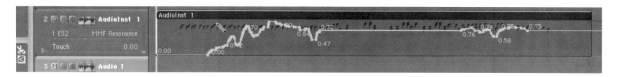

Freeze always starts at bar 1 and freezes to the end of the song. You can just stop
freezing when the SPL passes everything you want rendered.

Click on the Freeze icon. Press play. The Track will be rendered to disk.

If you want to abort the freeze, press the Apple and . (period) together. The portion of the track you have reached will be frozen, the rest of the track silenced.

Unfreezing a track

Just click on the Freeze icon to de-activate it. The Freeze will be undone.

Where are the rendered Freeze files?

The files are stored in the folder called 'Freeze Files' in the Logic folder. You may want to use these when creating an 'audio file' only Logic Song for loading into a computer with less CPU power or another type of recording software. You can decide what the format of the freeze files are in the Preferences>Audio window.

More CPU saving tips

- The more voices you use in an Instrument the more CPU power used. Use the Voices parameter to limit the number to the amount you actually need.
- Remember to de-instance plug-ins you are no longer using in a song.
- Use the Multi Channel version of the EXS24 sampler for a 25 piece drum kit rather than 25 instances of the stereo version.

The Internet | Appendix 2

The Internet is a major resource for information on

Virtual Instruments
Emagic Logic
Synthesisers
Physical Modelling
The Instruments modelled by Emagic

Along with

Mailing lists
Newsgroups

relating to the topics covered in this book.
  As the pages on the Internet are often transient, all that is provide here is a link

www.pc-publishing.com/logicinstruments.htm

where you will find an up to date list of useful internet resources.

Appendix 3 | MIDI control and automation

Most of Logic's Virtual Instruments parameters, can be adjusted by MIDI controllers. You'll find a list of these in the back of the manual for the Instrument if it supports this feature.

You may want to use a master keyboard or control surface with knobs and sliders that generate MIDI controller data. You'll usually find that you can define which MIDI controller number is sent out from which knob, button or slider on these devices. You'll need to check the manual to see how to do this.

Tip

Use Logic's transport to see the Controller numbers you are inputting into Logic when you turn a knob.

For example, the Filter Cutoff knob on the EXS24 responds to MIDI controller 89. If you set up a knob to output this MIDI controller, turning the physical knob on the hardware, say a Master keyboard, this will turn the virtual knob on the screen. This goes a long way to making the virtual instruments more 'hands-on' and more like their hardware counterparts. You could use a MIDI keyboard controller with several knobs to send out controller data to adjust the Filter Cutoff, Resonance and other Instrument controls all at the same time.

Automation

One of the advantages of using Emagic's own Virtual Instruments is their tight integration into Logic Audio. Every parameter that it's useful to automate, can be automated. This means that a song containing a Logic Virtual Instrument can be a very dynamic thing.

As an example let's look at ES2 automation. Open an Arrange page. Select Auto Track Zoom and Track Automation from the View menu. Select an Instrument Track and instance ES2 on the track

Info

For more information on automation within Logic Audio see the book 'Making Music with Emagic Logic Audio' by the same author.

208

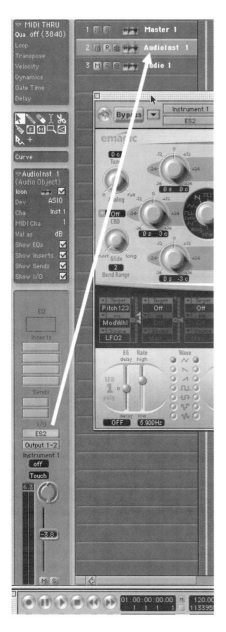

Select a nice sound from the preset menu. Play the ES2 and record the performance. Select Latch from the pull down menu.

Click on the Instrument list just under the AudioInst name. You'll see a pull down menu.

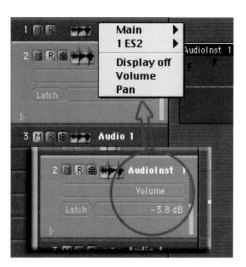

Look at the menu for the ES2 – you'll see the names of all the synthesiser's parameter that can be automated.

Select Volume from the menu.

Play back the sequence. While it's playing adjust the Filter cutoff. You'll see the data being written on the screen.

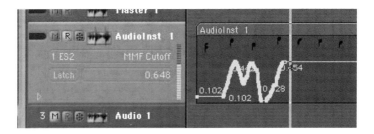

Adjust as many parameters as you like. Replay the track, adjust some more parameters. To see the automation data either;

1 Click on the Track as before to bring up the menu. Notice all the parameters that you've automated at the bottom of the menu. Select one. This the becomes then visible and is superimposed on the track, or

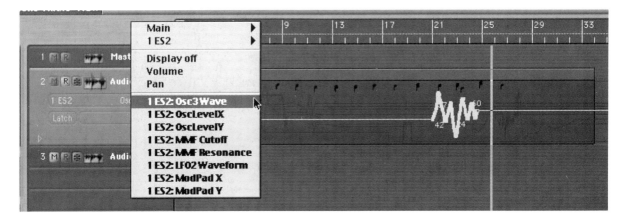

2 Click on the little triangle at the bottom of the Track. This will open another, automation track. Click on this Tracks triangle to expose more automation data until all automation tracks are exposed.

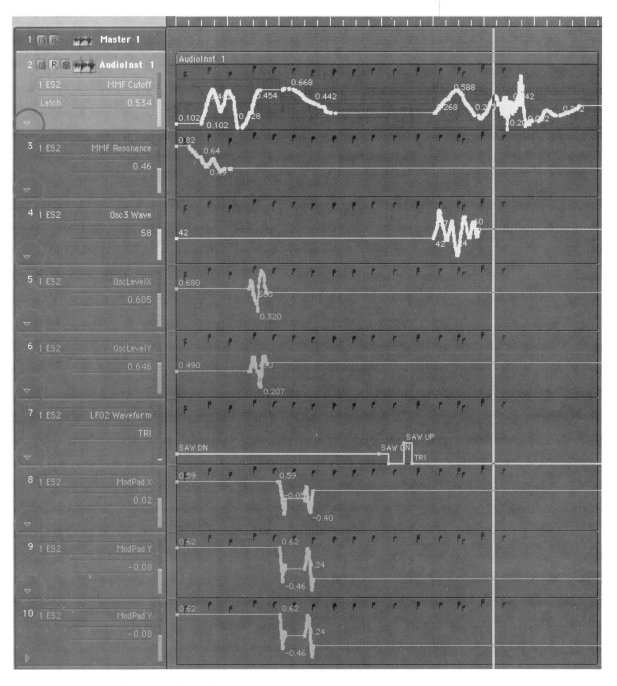

Automation data can then be edited with the mouse.

Appendix 4 | Further reading

Sound Synthesis with VST Instruments, Simon Millward, PC Publishing, ISBN 1870775732.

Making Music With Emagic Logic Audio, Stephen Bennett, PC Publishing, ISBN 1870775783.

Index

215

Making Music with
Emagic Logic Audio

Stephen Bennett

244 x 172 mm * 344 pages
ISBN 1870775 783

* For PC and Mac
* Installation and setting up
* Using the editors
* MIDI recording
* Recording audio
* Audio editing
* Plug-ins
* User tips and tricks

The book introduces all the features of Emagic Logic, but never loses sight of your objective – using the program to make great music. Emagic Logic is considered to be a complicated program, but, by taking a step by step logical approach, the book makes it easy to use the program's features to the full.

It describes the installation of the program on Macs and PCs, gives a practical introduction to setting up and using Logic, and it leads you through your first recording. It describes how to use the Arrange page, the Event list editor, the Matrix, Audio and Hyper editors, and how to use the Score editor to print out your music.

There are sections on audio and MIDI recording and editing, mixing, virtual instruments, mastering, plug-ins and audio processing. There is an invaluable overview of all the the menus in Logic, choosing and using a computer and audio interface for Logic, as well as lists of key commands and short-cuts.

In short it's all you need to get up and running with Emagic Logic!

PC Publishing
Export House, 130 Vale Road, Tonbridge, Kent TN9 1SP, UK
Tel 01732 770893 • Fax 01732 770268 • e-mail info@pc-publishing.com
Website http://www.pc-publishing.com

Check our website!
www.pc-publishing.com